Potter's Field 7

Novelette

31	Blood and Moondust by Mike Morgan

Short Stories

8	The Forgotten Man by H David Blalock
15	The Guardian by Tyree Campbell
67	The Galvanic by James Dorr
78	Night of the Nine Jack-o-Lanterns by Gary Davis
87	The Name-Us Game Counterpoint by Cecily Winter

Flash Fiction

97	Treasure by Margarida Brei

Poems

14	The Hounds of Hell by K. S. Hardy
27	They Didn't Tell by Gary Davis
30	Potter's Field 2020 by Denny E. Marshall
66	Solitary Potter's Field by Margarida Brei
76	Cinquains by Margarida Brei
77	The Majestic by Maureen Bowden
86	Scifaiku by Colleen Anderson
96	Vampire Girlz by Colleen Anderson
101	Love Unto the End by Colleen Anderson

102	Who's Who?

THE STAFF OF HIRAETH PUBLISHING

EDITOR: Tyree Campbell
WEBMASTER: H David Blalock
EDITORS:
Terrie Leigh Relf
Teri Santitoro
Marcie Lynn Tentchoff
H David Blalock
Bad Bob Bellam

Copyrights owned by the respective authors and artists
Cover art "Potter's Field" by Teri Santitoro
Cover design by Laura Givens

All rights reserved. No part of this book may be reproduced or transmitted in any form or by any means, electronic or mechanical, including photocopying or recording or by any information storage and retrieval systems, without expressed written consent of the author and/or artists.

Potter's Field 7 is a work of fiction. Names, characters, places, and incidents are products of the author's imagination. Any resemblance to actual events or persons, living or dead, is entirely coincidental.

First Printing, November 2021

Hiraeth Publishing
P.O. Box 1248
Tularosa, NM 88352
e-mail: hiraethsubs@yahoo.com

Visit www.hiraethsff.com for online science fiction, fantasy, horror, scifaiku, and more. Stop by our online bookstore for novels, magazines, anthologies, and collections. **Support the small, independent press...and your First Amendment rights.**

A Little Help, Please

In the world of the small indie press we fight a never-ending battle for attention to our work, as writers and in publishing. Here's an example: big publishers [you know who they are] have gobs of $$$ that they can devote to advertising and marketing. Here at Hiraeth Publishing, our advertising budget consists of the deposits for whatever soda bottles and aluminum cans we can find alongside the highways. Anti-littering laws make our task even more difficult . . . ☺

That's where YOU come in. YOU are our best promoter. YOU are the one who can tell others about us. Just send 'em to our website, tell them about our store. That's all. Just that.

Of course, we don't mind if you talk us up. We're pretty good, you know. We have some award-winning and award-nominated writers and artists, plus other voices well-deserving to be heard [not everyone wins awards, right?] but our publications are read-worthy nevertheless.

That number once again is:
www.hiraethsffh.com

Friend us on Facebook at Hiraeth Publishing
Follow us on Twitter at @HiraethPublish1

Annae (real name Maryjade) is an assassin sent to Deege, a forested world, to kill a plant and bring back the druzy who carries it. Druzies resemble young girls, but seem to have no life and no purpose but to act as transportation to the plants. In the process, Annae loses contact with her own spacecraft and is marooned on the world.

The man who hired Annae for this task is also responsible for the death of Annae's twin sister. Annae has accepted this contract because it presents an opportunity to kill the killer. However, the loss of the twin has crippled Annae. She is virtually unable to communicate with anyone, except in the course of negotiating her contracts. She has taken to talking with the memory of her dead sister, and with no one else.

Now, marooned on Deege, she must find a way to break out of her isolation and communicate with the druzies, and with a strange young woman who cannot speak, or she will be compelled to remain on this world forever.

https://www.hiraethsffh.com/product-page/becoming-jade-by-tyree-campbell

parABnormal Magazine

H. David Blalock, ed
SUBSCRIPTIONS

parABnormal Magazine is a print digest [trade paperback format] released quarterly by Hiraeth Publishing, in March, June, September, and December. *ParABnormal* publishes original stories, articles, art, reviews, interviews, and poetry.

The subject matter of *parABnormal Magazine* is, yes, the paranormal. For us, this includes ghosts, spectres, haunts, various whisperers, and so forth. It also includes shapeshifters, mythological creatures, and creatures from various folklores.

1-year subscription:
https://www.hiraethsffh.com/product-page/parabnormal-magazine-subscription

The Forgotten Man
H David Blalock

He no longer remembered his name. The drugs and alcohol had stolen it long ago. He only responded to "Emile" because people consistently called him by that name. He couldn't even remember if it truly was his or maybe it had been someone else's and he picked it up by mistake on one of those days he couldn't remember because of the drugs. It really didn't matter. "Emile" was just as good as any other name.

He lived, usually, in an otherwise abandoned building across from an abandoned building which in turn stood beside another abandoned building. He subconsciously identified with that abandonment. The buildings were old, used up, falling into ruin – just like Emile. Once they had been full of life, active and energetic, but time and bad decisions had left them bereft of all that – just like Emile.

So, though the buildings were cold and provided little shelter from the vagaries of the weather, though they were crumbling and unwanted, Emile felt at home within their dilapidated walls. They had become his safe place, away from the police who haunted his steps as he forged through bins and skips for food; away from the taunts and insults of children; away from the averted eyes and scowling disapproval of passersby as he sat on his corner, the cardboard sign propped against his knees that told them he once served his country and was wounded for his loyalty.

Before Iraq... It was as if he had been another person. He worked as an auto mechanic, delighting in the maintenance and upkeep of the latest offerings. From the simplicity of the undercarriage to the complexity of the computer monitoring and controls, he was fascinated by the dichotomy of 19th and 20th century technologies. After 9/11, he had been part of the patriotic response, volunteering to avenge the more than 3000 who lost their lives in the attack. He'd been proud to wear the uniform and they built on his expertise by assigning him to the base motor pool.

Then came the flight through Roosevelt Rhodes and on to the sands that invaded every gear and track and wheel just as if it were a living thing, as much an enemy to him and his work as the Iraqi forces. It had taken all his skill to keep those trucks, APCs, and other vehicles moving. It had been a full-time job that left him exhausted at shift end.

Maybe that was why he never found the time to write home, to check on his wife and daughter and how they were doing. The mail was fairly regular, not like it had been during Nam or Korea, he was sure. Still, it was two weeks old, the letter he got saying she had filed for divorce. She never explained why. And after a few months, he stopped wondering. He had his work and there was more than enough to keep his mind off home.

Home...

It was the same, and it was different. The people were different. He had never noticed how isolated people were from each other. He had become accustomed to the camaraderie of shared danger in the desert. When you're afraid you'll be killed at any moment, the people around you become more important to you. They are your brothers and sisters, all in the same situation, all looking out for each other. But here, at home...

No one seemed interested in hiring. There were too few jobs and too little money. And soon, there were too few family members. His parents died within six months of each other.

He lost his last connection to life. Life changed on him. Life at home was different. And the city...

Even the city seemed different. And that lack of connection, that coldness, had invaded it as well as the people.

A city is not just buildings, streets, and the people who live and work in it. A city is a living thing. It is born as a village, a settlement consisting of people gathered for mutual benefit or protection. It grows into a town as businesses begin providing more than the basic necessities. It finally becomes a city when people begin to become unhappy with it and start leaving for nearby villages and towns, creating suburbs.

The death of a city begins at its heart and works its way out. Much like a fairy ring, its center becomes used up and unable to support new growth. With proper management, the inner city, like the inside of the fairy ring, can be revived, but there will always be a band – ever expanding – of lifelessness. In cities, crime thrives within those fallow bands.

And that was where Emile found his place.

He was no master criminal. His expertise developed as a treasure finder, mostly treasures left in unlocked cars or discarded in hotel rubbish. The odd DVD or worn-out pair of shoes made good trade for the things he needed. He would sometimes find change in the street or parking lot near his building. In a good week, he might find as much is two dollars in dimes, nickels, and pennies. People seldom looked down as they walked to and from their cars. Going, they were more interested in their errand and sometimes were in such a hurry they would forget to lock their car. Coming, they were so concerned with their next task they would miss the change that fell from their pocket as they pulled out their keys or forget to look around them as they got into the car and didn't see the wallet fall out as they slid into their seat. Parking lots were prime areas for finding treasure.

The police knew him at sight. He had no place to hide from them. Occasionally, an officer would pull up outside his building and look in on him. He liked to think they were concerned about his health, but knew their visits coincided more with local burglaries. He had no ill will toward them about that. It was their job. He understood. He just wished they called him something other than "you" or "old man." He had a name, though it might have been borrowed. They could have made the effort to ask.

In the winter of what he thought was his 63rd year on Earth and his 21st on the streets, Emile found a ring in the parking lot of the nearby hotel. It was a woman's ring, gold with diamonds in tiny clusters around its circumference. His sight was no longer what it had been, but he could make out markings on its inner surface that could be letters, perhaps an inscription. An engagement or wedding ring, perhaps.

Emile looked around. There was no one else in the parking lot. Such a ring would not simply slip off someone's finger. It could have fallen out of a pocket or purse... But surely it would quickly be missed. Maybe the woman had taken it off out of a fit of pique and thrown it away? It looked new, as if it had not been worn long. Whatever the truth might be, he found himself in possession of something that could change his life.

He gazed at the ring and realized what it meant – to the person who lost it, because certainly it had been discarded, but mostly to himself. He could pawn it or, better yet, trade it for something big. He smiled as he considered the possibilities. Food, some decent clothes, maybe even a soft bed for a night or two. Maybe his luck had finally changed. Maybe his finding this ring was only the first in a line of fortunate events that would put him back on track to a normal life, a life he had thought forever lost.

He felt a long-forgotten warmth as the ring turned in his fingers. The diamonds glittered their magic and his mind responded with dreams of returning prosperity.

"Oh, thank God!"

Emile started. He looked around to see a young woman, eyes red and swollen from crying, standing close by and looking at him. Dressed in blue and obviously for a special event, she was a reminder of someone he had once known... someone he once thought would be his future.

"Please," she said as she cautiously approached. "It's my sister's wedding ring. I dropped it. I was running late. I..." She stopped. "May I have it back, please?"

Emile stared at her, trying to put together her words. He could see the distress in her eyes, the growing fear that he wouldn't surrender the ring. Distress and fear: two emotions he knew only too well.

But why should he give it up? Her sister could get married without it. He remembered being married once a long time ago, before the drugs, before the alcohol. There had even been... A child? Yes, a little girl. He remembered her looking at him with distress and fear. He shook his head at that memory. The woman must have thought he was denying her.

"Please!" she cried, tears forming in her eyes. She swung her purse off her shoulder and shoved it at him. "Take this. Take it all. There's cash and credit cards. I won't report them for a week. I need that ring! Please!"

Emile stared at the purse, then the ring. He thought about the little girl, could hear her voice as she pleaded for him not to go to Iraq, to stay home. Tears welled up in his own eyes as he remembered the letter telling him about the auto accident that had stilled that little voice forever. His legs failed him and he sank to his knees, trying to shut out the memory of the tiny coffin, the sharp accusations from his soon-to-be ex.

"I'm sorry," he sobbed. "So sorry."

He dropped the ring, staggered to his feet, and ran.

He ran to escape the past, to stop the voice calling for him not to go. He ran until he couldn't run another step and collapsed on the sidewalk, eyes tightly shut and hands on his ears, but the voice still sounded in his mind, the sight of the little girl's face stayed clear in his head. No matter what he did, he couldn't escape that vision, the manifestation of his guilt and regret.

If only he hadn't gone, if only he'd taken the offered position in town as a recruiter instead, maybe she wouldn't have died. Maybe his ex-wife was right. Maybe he went to Iraq to escape his responsibilities at home.

"Get up," a gruff voice growled. "You can't stay here. Move along."

Emile came to his senses to find himself lying on the sidewalk in front of one of the city's many strip joints. A huge bald man dressed in black hauled him bodily to his feet and shoved him away from the door.

"Get lost," the bouncer snapped.

Emile shrank away, holding his hands up against possible attack. The man watched, scowling, as Emile stumbled down the street.

"Sober up, asshole!" the bouncer shouted after him before going back inside.

But Emile *was* sober, and that was his problem. Only when the drugs loosed their hold did that haunting memory return.

Several blocks away, he stumbled over a kindred doomed soul. The city streets were full of homeless here, living off scraps and sheltered by makeshift tents and hovels of cardboard and debris.

The man Emile found would suffer no more. He was cold and stiff from something other than weather. Eventually, the police would find him and he would become just another John Doe to populate a box in a potter's field. To Emile, though, he was a resource. The clothes were too ragged, the pockets empty of everything except...

It was white, crystalline, and promised forgetfulness. There was enough there, more than enough, to stop the memories forever

He cradled it in his hands, closed his eyes, and put it in his mouth.

"I'm sorry," was his last coherent thought.

The Hounds of Hell
K. S. Hardy

Long dead from run over
Or hypodermics full of sleep
And buried in secret places
They have been called forth
With still wicked sharp teeth
And black claws with which
To rend flesh from bone,
And swift to the killing
At the asking of their
New master's evil voice,
The devil dogs prowl the dark,
Eyes aglow with Hades's fire
Awaiting their age-old task
To hunt down wandering souls
That refuse the final rest.

The Guardian
Tyree Campbell

You won't find *La Caleta de la Sangre de Ladrones* on any modern map of Costa Rica, but it's there just the same, an inconspicuous notch in the coastline of the *Bahía de Coronado*, just south of the mouth of the great river that plunges from the cordillera to the Pacific. You might be able to locate it on a geodesic survey map, but it won't be named. The local fishermen know it well, this "Thieves' Blood Cove," if you can get them to talk about it. They seldom accommodate strangers—live ones, at least.

I'd arrived expatriate some years back from a small town in western Oregon, a young teacher of French who, one very warm spring, had remained after classes with Annie Rae Johnson to conjugate several irregular verbs. I had a passport and enough cash to get me away from the outcries and onto a Peruvian fishing boat headed south. When I'd had enough of the gutting and scaling, the chum and the nets, they kindly put me ashore in Domenical, a town that *is* on the map, about sixty kilometers north of this two-room thatch and stone hut where I now write by sunlight and candlelight.

By the time I worked my way south to this settlement around Thieves' Blood Cove I still had some cash but nothing to spend it on. The villagers caught fish and smoked it, and when the government boat came round every two months or so they exchanged it for this and that —food, fabric, clothing, netting, the odd implement. The *guardacostales* never, ever, came ashore, and refused to accept money from the villagers, only barter. I thought this odd at the time, but subsequent events have invested me with an understanding that I would not have wished on anyone. From the littoral forest the villagers gathered fruits and nuts and tubers, lizards and rodents and large cockroaches—almost enough, with the fish they held back, to feed almost everyone. I was an unwelcome extra mouth. The village children had no need for French, but my Spanish was passable, thanks to the Peruvian fishermen, and some of the parents wanted their youngsters to read. That, I could teach.

Thus the beach sand became paper, and sticks pencils. I ran an egalitarian classroom, ignorance a leveler despite the range of ages of the students. I feared their minimal skills would fail them from disuse, but sometimes the *guardacostales* on the boats brought with them old newspapers with comic strips, and tattered books, and even some comic books. Whenever it rained, which at times was almost daily, the class and I took refuge under the forest canopy to preserve the reading material. That's where I found the crosses.

We were sitting at the base of a mahogany tree that must have taken root about the time Coronado stopped by the bay that now bears his name, encircled by a gray curtain of rain that fell so hard it raised a mist all around us that reminded me of the impenetrable fog along the Oregonian coast. The connection with my past saddened me briefly. In flight I had abandoned a technology luxurious in contrast to this primitive jungle, and a level of civilization to which I might never return. Already I missed radios and cars and toiletries and M&Ms, items I would have thought surely the village could afford one or two of. But I had not thrown away the key to my way back . . . not yet. That would come later.

As the rain flattened groundcover and bent fronds, I chanced to look in the direction of a tiny cleared plot some ten meters inland from us, where I could just make out the four crosses, indistinct as an Impressionist's painting —and for a moment I doubted the evidence of my eyes. The village had no cemetery, after all, and funerals were conducted in Puerto Cortés, on the north bank of the great river. What, then, could this be?

José, sitting on the groundcover and mud beside me, his thin body hunkered over the comic books to shield them from the drops that sieved through the canopy of mahogany and palm, noticed where I was looking, and averted his eyes. At twelve, he was old enough to relate the settlement's simpler rumors and tales. "What is that place, José?" I asked, over the dull roar of the torrent.

He knew very well what I was asking, and did not look. "*¿Quién sabe, Señor? Es muy antigua.*"

"*How* old?"

"*No hay santos allí, Señor.*"

An unexpected *frisson* shook me. *There is nothing holy there*, José had averred. His tone pleaded with me to ask no more of him. I glanced at the other four children. None had eyes for the burial site, not even the ingenuous six-year-old Felipe. Whatever was there frightened them into silence and avoidance at a very early age, and I pressed the matter with them no further.

When the rain stopped and the children returned to the village, I remained behind. Without the pressure of the falling water, the fronds and branches had risen back into place, all but obscuring the burial site. Over spongy terrain I crept, nudging foliage out of the way with my machete, until I could proceed no further without hacking away the obstructions. This I was reluctant to do—one avoids making unnecessary noise in cemeteries—but curiosity overwhelmed that subliminal taboo. Furthermore, in the back of my mind lurked the notion that somewhere in the dense forest beyond the four crosses squatted previously unknown pre-Mayan structures, containing perhaps treasures of gold and jade that had eluded the greedy clutches of Cortés and Coronado.

But the pre-Columbian civilizations of Central America did not mark the remains of their dead with crosses. If others had died previously in search of local treasures, I needed to exercise caution. I slashed at branches and fronts, gently at first, then with vigor as the heavy sharp blade passed almost soundlessly through rain-drenched wood pulp, putting to rest my earlier concerns about making enough noise to wake the dead. Presently I was standing at the edge of the cleared area.

Not crosses.

Three were empty scabbards, broken and tied to cruciforms. The fourth was a broadsword, its heavy blade patched with rust the way lichen grows on granite, and stuck about halfway into the ground. Centuries of tropical rains had eroded away the mounds marked by the makeshift crosses, but I thought it odd that vegetation did not cover the gravesite. Beneath my bare feet mud yielded, the sensation rather like walking through yogurt, and I jumped back, fearing I might sink all the way down to the encased remains . . . or more chilling, the remains themselves. Supported once again by groundcover, I reached for the sword, grasped it by the haft, and paused. A mad notion flashed through my mind: that, after the fashion of Arthur, I was about to become King of the Isthmus. At my bark of laughter, a scarlet and yellow bird flew from a tree, protesting raucously.

I pulled on the sword and easily it came free of the mud. Nothing much else happened. There did pass an eerie moment when I was sure I heard the hiss of escaping air and a gurgling sound, but this came from the mud and water that spilled into the space vacated by the sword, and when the hole had been filled, the sounds stopped.

Stuck to the tip of the sword was a gold coin: a doubloon, from the look of it, and shiny as though freshly minted.

Silence fell in that moment like a hammer. Birds and lizards and insects seemed to pause, as if regarding me with bated breaths: what would I do next? I felt eyes on me, and heard soft whispers through the leaves and fronds, though there was no one about. Gradually I became aware of the slow steady drip of raindrops from a frond nearby into a small puddle at the base of a massive tree. The splashes seemed to keep pace with my heartbeat, accelerated now as it coursed adrenalin through my body. Although the message of fear had yet to reach my conscious thoughts, I was afraid.

I envisioned my next move: tuck the coin into a pocket, and later, when no one was watching, come back with a shovel, perhaps to uncover a cache of gold coin. Against this eminently practical response to a find of gold, I felt a powerful impulse to ram the sword back into the ground and forget I had ever visited the gravesite. *Run*, said my brain. *Flee*. But the doubloon glittered sunlight into my eyes, and it became in that moment all I could see. With the gold, I might escape from here, I might buy my way back to civilization. I might even set myself up on a *hacienda* somewhere, away from anyone who might still be looking for me. Argentina, maybe, with all that good beef and all those *señoritas*. The gold was my ticket. I reached for it. The feel of the coat of arms and the letters raised by the strike confirmed through my fingertips the reality of what had been a surreal moment.

The coin was real: wet, warm, and alive.

It was mine.

I plucked the coin from the tip of the sword and quickly slipped it into my pocket. I looked around. Had anyone seen me? The surrounding forest was quiet still, its denizens watching. I felt their eyes on me. I thrust the sword back into the ground, to make it appear as though nothing had transpired here. The blade slid through the muck and struck something solid, something hard. A treasure chest? Whatever the sword had struck had yielded slightly. Not a treasure chest, then. But what? I withdrew the sword again.

And found another doubloon.

It was easy to imagine a horde of coins buried some two feet under the surface. Once more I plunged the sword into the ground . . . and felt a tug at my elbow. I yelped. My feet actually left the ground. Heretofore I had thought such a response to sudden fright merely an exaggeration. But I literally leapt into the air.

It was José. The expression on his face was a blend of loathing and fear, and I could not tell whether these were directed at me and what I was doing, or at the gravesite. I swore under my breath, at him and at the world, and tried to stabilize my heart rate with several slow and steady inhalations.

Still grasping my elbow, José looked up at me. "¿*Cuántos quiere matar, Señor*?" he asked. "How many of us do you wish to kill?"

It took a moment for the question to sink in, so unexpected it was. The moment of discovery was shattered. In the trees, birds resumed their calls, and small animals scurried once more. The forest returned to its vegetative state.

"I don't know what you mean, José," I said, the guilt of two gold doubloons weighing in my pocket.

"Come back to the village, *Señor*." Again he tugged at me. Evidently he had not seen me tuck the two coins away.

In my mind's eye I saw a Charles Dickens scene, a little boy begging his father to come home from the tavern. It wasn't the same thing as José and I—and again the guilt of the gold rang against my thigh. I let him lead me back toward the ocean and out of the forest, thinking that if I came with him, I would come home from the tavern. He left me at my hut, and would not look back. I had disappointed him.

* * *

That evening no one brought me dinner, nor was I invited to partake of the common meal. Word had gotten out about my little foray into the forest. I felt it imprudent to inquire after the duration of the ostracism, but surely they did not intend that I starve to death. I paced the sandy floor of my hut to the occasional heavy chime of two gold doubloons. How had they come to be in this place? Pirate treasure, surely—but which pirate? Most had operated in the Caribbean. I recalled that Cocos Island, which belonged to Costa Rica, was once a repository for treasure, most of which had not been found. Some names came to me: Edward Davis, Francis Drake, Benito Bonito. But Drake took his back to England. Davis's consisted mainly of gold bars. The doubloons, then, might have belonged to Bonito. Or to someone else entirely. I couldn't see that it mattered.

In due time the Pacific Ocean swallowed the sun for the night. I expected to hear a hiss as the ruddy orb touched the water, but there was hardly any sound at all. Even the deaths of the waves on the sand were muted. Nor did I hear any voices emanating from the other huts. I had the sudden, horrible thought that something out there might be attracted to the sounds of the village. Or perhaps to the lights. I doused my candle and sat on the sand floor of the hut and listened to the sounds of the night.

Thieves' Blood Cove had fallen silent as starlight.

The luminescence from the breaking waves and the light from the stars themselves cast the forest and beach in flickering that came alive. Something spectral and fleeting emerged from the forest, drifting over the sand and desiccated seaweed without making a sound. Had I believed in wraiths, I might have thought this one, though it possessed no distinct shape. In the darkness of the hut I dared not move. My eyes followed the specter across the open doorway and window until it passed from the line of my sight. Presently the afterglow of its passing faded.

As softly as possible, I let out a sigh of relief . . . and drew a huge breath as a scream shattered the silence.

I crawled to the window and peered out into the night. One of the perimeter huts had ignited in a blue-white aura, and through its window I saw movement. Wailing began, a ululating shriek that reached its crescendo just as a glowing figure emerged from the hut, a writhing child in each arm. My mind's eye made the figure a pirate, for such was my only frame of reference. Behind, on her knees, crept a woman, her hands clenched together in ferocious supplication. At last she fell, still shrieking, tearing at her hair with one hand while she pounded her breast with the other.

Two children. Two coins.

The ghost pirate, if such it was, merged with the forest, still clutching the children. More screams reached my ears: of the children, but of something else in the forest, something primordial and elemental. Presently the screaming ceased the way the sound of a passing train dopplers out, and the only sound on the beach was that of the woman keening.

Although no one else was about, I felt the eyes of the village on me. Involuntarily I hunched my shoulders against their accusation and withdrew into my darkness. Sleep came and went fitfully, filled with shapeless dreads.

* * *

Morning came without warning, startling me awake. I had slept late. Already the villagers were gathering driftwood, netting fish, plucking fruit, and mending clothes and roofs. I scarcely had time to rub the film from my teeth before the sound of chittering announced the arrival of José and the other children for their reading lesson. At my beckon they gathered around the walls of the hut and waited until I had rinsed and run fingers through my hair, dislodging old bits of kelp and grains of sand. Only my memory suggested that the night had not passed peacefully.

After the lesson José remained behind. He sat cross-legged in the corner on the sandy floor, his face partially concealed by shadows that made him look years older. He seemed to be collecting himself. I reckoned he had been selected by the villagers to convey their condemnation for my crime. For too long a time he did not speak, so I gave him a nudge.

"What's on your mind, José?" I asked, as I sat down on an old log.

He looked at me through unruly black locks and made up his mind. "Alvaro will come for you, *Señor*."

"I'll put them back."

"There is no need, *Señor*. They have been paid for."

"Then why—-?"

"You are not of us, *Señor*," said José, as if that explained everything.

Much more I wanted to ask him, but in that moment one of the villagers peered into the hut and crooked an insistent finger at José. He was one of the elders, Rodrigo by name, round of head and body and swarthy of complexion, with a yellow-brown beard that he kept neatly trimmed. Both departed, leaving me to my own devices. I decided to be proactive, and take my case to the forest and the gravesite, overriding the objections from my pounding heart. It was after all daylight, and ghosts only came out at night. Or so I supposed.

* * *

The terrain along the approach to the gravesite was still spongy from the previous day's rainfall, but that was the only familiarity. It seemed to me that the fronds and branches I had hacked out of my way had grown back in the interim, as if to re-establish the boundary around the unholy site. I had brought along my machete, although I questioned its efficacy against spectral armaments, and employed it once again to clear my way. Presently, sweating in torrents, I reached the crosses and the muck into which they had been driven.

The gold doubloons weighed against my pocket like sins upon a soul. I had come to this place without any particular plan, but now I understood—or thought I understood—what I had to do. I withdrew one coin, my thumb finding the hole the sword had made, then pulled the rusty broadsword from the mud. Affixed to the sword point was a third gold coin, thwarting my plan. I stood there, stumped as if by a puzzle, trying to grasp what I had done and what I had to do now.

My mind was a blank. All around me, the forest had fallen quiet as once again its denizens peered down at me, waiting to see what I would do next.

In one hand I clutched a gold coin, in the other a pirate's sword. The shutter of Time clicked, recording my appearance in that forever moment as evidence of my complicity in a crime I did not yet fathom.

Time had stopped. The forest remained silent. Above me, brightly feathered necks craned to gain a better view of the tableau. I might have heard an eyelid blink, so quiet it was.

From somewhere above the graves I heard a drip drip drip. The cadence matched that of my heartbeat. Slowly I raised my eyes in that stilled time, until I saw the black hair dangling straight down. Drops of liquid beaded along the tresses, gathered at the bottom, and then fell one by one into the mud perhaps ten feet below—the mud in which I was now standing.

I looked up.

The faces were next, pale in the shadows of the trees, eyes wide and seeing nothing in this world. Then came the necks, a raw gash across each, and in those gashes pooled the very last of the blood they had released.

Drip drip drip.

Clothes I saw, ragged and also blooded. Arms had been bound behind backs. Trousers hung limply around the legs, which had also been tied together. Two ropes, one around each pair of ankles, secured the corpses to overhanging branches.

With the sins that weighed upon my soul came an overwhelming sorrow. *No!* In the name of God, *why?*

I closed my eyes, bringing an end to the reality of that moment, but not the everlasting memory of it.

Then the next moment came to pass, and its silence was broken by a gravelly voice from just beyond the gravesite. "You cannot put them back," I heard, and turned, swallowing the stone that my heart had suddenly become, to find the source of the words.

He wore all the trappings of a pirate out of Hollywood, from the cocked black tricorn to the thigh-high Wellingtons, from the leather belt that held his black trousers in place to the previously white shirt, now beige with age, that fit him loosely, and to the cutlass that he held in his right hand.

His black beard and rough appearance matched stereotypes. Only his eyes made him real. Blue as glacial ice they were, and as cold. But not dead, no, not dead. His eyes were alive and on fire.

If ghost he was, he was also palpable.

"Alvaro," I said.

"It is unseemly for a thief to attempt to return what he has stolen." Here he raised his cutlass, the heavy blade gleaming in the shafts of sunlight that had managed to penetrate the canopy. "Have you no honor, sir?"

I hefted the two coins. "I thought perhaps—-"

"Those are yours. You took them fair." Alvaro gestured upwards with his cutlass. "Those whose part it was to guard the booty have been punished."

Sickness coarsened my voice as I looked up. "They had nothing to do with this."

"They are part of the village." Now he pointed at the broadsword I held, and at the doubloon at the tip of it. "Another must now be punished."

"No more children, Alvaro." I tried to plunge the sword back into the mud, but it would not go. It was as if the mud had turned to brick.

"The coin is yours," said Alvaro. "You must take it, ladrón. That is the way of it."

I shook my head, and tried again. "You will slaughter another child."

"Whoever is chosen is already dead, ladrón." He lifted his tricorn, presenting a clearer view of his face, and leaned against a tree. I expected him to fall right through it, but he proved to be an entity of substance. Yet he could not be so. I recalled José's caution earlier: *There is nothing holy here.* "This is the way of it," said Alvaro, and proceeded to tell me.

* * *

The gold, said Alvaro de Silva, had been brought ashore by himself, a lieutenant who had been entrusted with this task by the pirate Benito Bonito. The reason was simple enough: the pirates, fearing the squadron of English warships that had just arrived in the area to suppress piracy, did not want to be caught with the loot. Therefore, Alvaro and his rowboat of men were to cache the booty for pick-up later, after the English had departed. Already the English had begun to fire on Bonito's ship, and smoke soon rose from her blasted decks. Alvaro and his men could only watch helplessly as the attack progressed. It seemed to Alvaro that two or three of Bonito's vessels were escaping, but smoke and mist shrouded the outcome.

On shore there was a falling-out. One faction wanted to take the gold inland and keep it for themselves; the other, led by Alvaro, held to their orders from Bonito to protect the treasure. Alvaro and three others who had maintained their loyalty to Bonito survived the fighting. The rowboat, however, was destroyed. The four men were stranded.

Certain that Bonito would quickly realize what must have happened, Alvaro did not expect to remain on shore for very long. So they waited. Days passed, and weeks, months, yet the four survivors never lost faith, nor shirked their duties. In due time, they took up with native women, who were made gifts to them by a tribe living inland, in return for assurances that the men had no designs on the tribal village. They built a village and raised families, and taught their children to honor Bonito's orders. All swore oaths never to allow thieves to take the treasure, even after death.

Even after death Alvaro and his three comrades continued to guard the Bonito gold. No one had come to relieve them.

The village remained small and squalid. The gold might have bought amenities and a better life, but oaths had been sworn. The site itself soon gained a reputation as a harbor for the ghosts of thieves who had dishonored their captain, and was avoided. The *guardacostales* saw to the village as they saw to the others along the coastline but, fearing the evil spirits, never came ashore.

Time passed, and the four men of Bonito waited, waited for orders, waited to be relieved. Three times during the ensuing decades a stray outsider arrived, adventurer or refugee. Three times the cache site was discovered, and the crosses that marked it. Three times the village was punished for its perfidy. Three dead strays relieved Alvaro's three comrades.

Leaving Alvaro himself.

You are not of us, Señor, José had said.

"This is the site where we fought," said Alvaro. "The blood of thieves courses through these roots, these veins, forever." He glanced up. "As does the blood of the children of thieves, for in the end, that is what we are, each and all. We took from the world, and you have come to take from us."

"No more children, Alvaro."

"As you wish," he said.

His cutlass moved faster than the sunlight it reflected. I felt a tug at my throat, nothing more. *Whoever is chosen is already dead*, Alvaro had said. Already he had begun to fade from view, having been relieved at long last. In his place, three other specters were taking shape.

At my feet a puddle of blood began to form, thick and rich. If I listened carefully, I could hear a steady drip drip drip.

They Didn't Tell
Gary Davis

Stars in the chill void of space
bear witness from infinity.

Clouds thousands of feet high
sail and blow by leisurely.

Frothing tides roll in and roll out,
wet and dry this small rocky isle.

Crabs and critters scamper and dig.
They leave naught but a sandy pile.

Below earth and sky, silence runs deep.
Ten dead pirates, forgotten they sleep.

Can You See Me?
By M. R. Williamson

After falling ill from a fever, Susan's parents put her in their car to go to the doctor. Along the way, a blowout causes the car to crash, killing the parents, who are unaware that their daughter had already died back at the house.

Every morning after the accident, Susan awakens in her upstairs bedroom to await the return of her parents. Time passes, and the house gains a spooky reputation that makes it almost impossible to sell. Prospective clients have been unable to cope with the mysterious goings-on . . . until now.

https://www.hiraethsffh.com/product-page/can-you-see-me-by-m-r-williamson

Potters Field 2020

Denny E. Marshall

On the edge of town
At the end of pine lake road
Is a new potters field
Called covid
The souls cry out
From rows of mass graves
Buried together
Yet all alone
At midnight and full moons
They walk around in confusion
Their emptiness blinds them
From the torch of the gate
Never having a chance
For the hold of last goodbyes
Tears miles apart
Like orphans
All the families
Hoping for better answers
Waiting for the light
At the end of the tunnel
While death keeps counting
Unto the new year

Blood and Moondust
Mike Morgan

"You must have something embarrassing in your past," asked Daphne's crewmate. "Something you cringe at the thought of, even now."

She didn't answer straight away, being busy at the controls. Commander Daphne Guillory hadn't flown a Kestrel to the Moon for thirteen years. No one had, on account of manned spaceflight being universally abandoned. Yet here she was, undertaking another mission, called back into service because she met several stringent requirements: she'd been a great spacecraft pilot, she had a flight-ready medical status, and she was still alive. All this because Space Command needed to urgently ascertain how its long-abandoned Moonbase Gamma had inexplicably switched itself back on.

They hadn't jumped directly to sending people. Their first response had been a robot probe. It had malfunctioned thirty seconds after lunar arrival. It was then Command had decided to assemble a crew to investigate. A small one, though. Due to the likely danger, only two qualified personnel. Daphne had not hesitated to accept the mission.

The experts in the administration had a theory about the 'how' of the base's reanimation. They'd shared it with Daphne shortly before the Kestrel's departure. She didn't buy their cockamamy idea for one second. If they really believed what they'd claimed and, what's more, if that were their justification for casting aside decades of effort in sending humanity beyond the Earth, she honestly feared for their sanity.

As for the 'why,' no one had a clue. Finding that out was top of the list of priorities she'd been given.

"I guess," she admitted, having thought her crewmate's question over. "Why do I have to go first?"

"Because your stories are funnier than mine," answered the man sat on the other side of the cockpit. Her teammate in the Kestrel was Rashidi Onyilogwu, a systems specialist from Kenya who, like her, had survived from the glory days of space exploration.

Space Command had not shared their theories with him. Doing so, they said, was not absolutely necessary for Rashidi to perform his function. To minimize the risk of exposing the real reason why humanity had retreated from the stars, the secret was kept to as few people as possible. The governments of the world didn't want to panic their populations. Therefore, she was under orders not to tell him. The command struck her as being every bit as absurd as the so-called secret itself.

While Daphne had brushed up her flying skills on simulators in the weeks leading up to launch, Rashidi had used 3-D holo-schematics from the archive to reacquaint himself with the base's infrastructure and equipment. Now, two days into the journey from Earth to the Moon, and closing rapidly on their target, they were about to discover whether their hurried preparations had been extensive enough.

"Fine," she said. "When I was a teenager, my folks got live-in jobs at a historic mansion. Free rent, but they had to reenact nineteenth century daily life every weekend for the tourists. Full costumes, cheesy dialogue, the works."

"Don't see how that's embarrassing." Two days of sharing the cramped quarters of the Kestrel and they'd worked their way through all the normal conversational topics. They knew all about each other's families, where they'd gone to school, what they'd studied at college. They were left with obscurer subjects to pass the remaining time.

"I was roped in, too. You know, volun-told to help out, to be an example of what a thirteen-year-old privileged white girl in the 1910s in Louisiana would've been like." She ran a diagnostics check to prepare for the landing cycle.

"Still not seeing the toe-curling horror of it."

If finding a crew versed in the obsolete skills of space travel had been hard, putting together a functional launch vehicle had been harder. Fortunately, Kestrels had once been the workhorses of the world's space effort and hundreds had been manufactured. The vehicles were reusable, reconfigurable for multitudes of purposes, and built on a production line to be cheap. At least, they had been, back in the days when people flew into the void. Those factory lines had stood idle for a long time now. Assembling this vehicle had required parts from twenty-six decommissioned Kestrels. Thank God the fleet had been sent out to rust in a desert in Nevada and not broken up all those years ago; otherwise, they would never have collected the necessary components in such a short time.

Daphne sighed, waiting for the diagnostic results. "My school sent the seventh grade on field trips to the mansion every year. So, when I turned thirteen, it was my class's turn to go. My parents figured it would be super neat for me to do my usual turn as a reenactor in front of my friends. My teacher agreed with them."

Rashidi shrugged. "That does sound fun, actually."

The computer flashed up the results of the systems check. "We're good for descent," she reported back to Space Command. "Estimate five minutes to touchdown on pad eight."

Ground control acknowledged her transmission and wished them luck. An unusual degree of static cut across the exchange, making it hard for her to hear their reply.

To Rashidi, she said, "You remember what it's like to be thirteen?"

"You were shy?" he guessed.

Daphne told hold of the steering handle in case the automatics failed. "Uh-huh." The Moon's landscape turned under them, the wall of a crater passing by. She caught sight of the moonbase through the Kestrel's window. Earthlight reflected off the metal blocks of the surface buildings. Landing pads dotted the base's perimeter, each one kept a safe distance from critical structures in case of a disastrous landing or departure. "It was bad enough I had to do it at all, let alone in front of my classmates."

"They weren't kind?"

"They were not," she confided, as the Kestrel fired retroes for final approach. There were lights on inside the landing pad's side building, shining out through the thick windows. From Rashidi's expression, he saw them too. So much for the base being shut down. That proved it—the anomalous data received by the ground monitoring stations was accurate. There was something weird going on. It remained to be seen whether it was exact variety of weird predicted by the experts.

A ring of lights turned on, marking the edge of the pad, as they descended. Moondust blew in every direction. "Ground, we're seeing evidence of multiple electrical systems in operation." The verbal report was redundant given they were broadcasting video footage but hearing them answer made Daphne feel better. Again, static hissed over their dispassionate reply.

"Gotta be intruders," breathed Rashidi. That seemed likely. A damn sight more likely than the alternative. Someone must have turned the power back on. But who were they, and how had they reached the base when no one left the Earth anymore?

Her colleague added in a louder voice, "Was that when you decided you had to get away, when they all laughed at you?"

"Yeah. Figured outer space was just about enough distance."

The Kestrel lurched as its landing gear made contact with the pad. The whine of the engines died down. Rashidi tapped at his controls. "The skywalk is extending from the terminal building. There's definitely main power in the base. We should have door seals established in a few seconds."

"Let's suit up."

Just because there was power there was no guarantee the base's air supply had been restored, even assuming the facility was still capable of holding an atmosphere. Daphne wasn't going to trust any air sensors in the base, either, no matter what they claimed. They might have been interfered with. As far as she was concerned, pressurized suits were the best way of staying alive.

The two of them hoisted themselves out of their flight seats, and took careful, low-g steps into the craft's main section. They shrugged on orange one-piece outfits and attached white backpacks containing air cannisters. Golden helmets went on last.

"Well," said Daphne, looking out through her visor at Rashidi's orange-clad form. "Let's go find out what the hell's going on."

The doors of the Kestrel's main compartment slid aside, revealing a silent, empty corridor. She holstered a sidearm and stepped through, Rashidi close behind.

***

Most of the mile-wide base was underground. The structures visible from the surface were the tips of metal icebergs submerged in lunar regolith, all the better to protect the base's inhabitants from radiation exposure. Daphne and Rashidi wasted no time crossing the skywalk to the landing pad's terminal and bounding down the ramp to the first of these subterranean levels.

To Daphne's relief, the lower level was just as well-lit as the surface one. No need to use the suits' lights. The situation was unsettling enough without having to stumble around in the dark with only a couple of shoulder-mounted flashlights to show their surroundings. Another blessing: the lower floor was as devoid of life as the upper level. It was a waiting area, cluttered with white plastic furniture designed in that curving, no-sharp-angles style so beloved of facilities where people wore suits they didn't want to tear.

She tried to call in their progress. All she heard was that pernicious static, louder than ever. "I can't raise Ground."

"There were no indications of sunspot activity. We should be getting a clear signal, relayed through our Kestrel."

"Interference of some kind?"

"There's nothing here that could cause that," Rashidi answered.

Daphne knew what he meant. When the base had been closed down, the personnel on the final Kestrels out had executed Operation Exodus, stripping the facility of every last piece of electronic equipment, barring the wiring in the walls and a few monitors. Nothing dangerous had been left behind, nothing that could fall into the wrong hands in some future decade and be misused.

That was the official story, at least. She was sure a few processors and network switches had been overlooked, simply because of the scale of the undertaking. As far as equipment that could jam radio went, it would be true enough, though. Which meant that if their signals were being interfered with, that jamming gear had been brought up to the Moon recently. More evidence that the base had been broken into.

Rashidi must have been thinking the same as her, because she could see through his visor his lips forming a thin line. "We go on?"

"We have to. We're here to figure out what's happening and report back. If need be, we can transmit our findings from lunar orbit." Contact with mission control during the reconnaissance would be nice, but they were two hundred forty thousand miles away. Even with normal communications, there wasn't much they could do if she and Rashidi got into trouble.

"Very well. I'll run checks on central systems. See what's what."

Rashidi moved to a wall and removed a panel. He soon had a tablet hooked up to the base's cabling. "You know, it's odd," he said.

"What is?"

"We can't contact Earth, but we can transmit to each other." He turned to look at her. "Our suit comms broadcast via radio as well. If one channel is being blocked, why aren't both of them?"

"You're saying there's no logic to it."

"I am. And there's no logic to what I'm registering on my pad, either."

"What do you mean?"

Instead of explaining, he gestured at the glowing inset wall panels with his gloved hand. "You agree the lights are blazing away."

Where was he going with this? "We can see they are."

"Neat trick, considering there's no current in these power lines."

"That's impossible."

"No one repaired and replenished the main power reactor, commander. It's not active. None of these systems are drawing electricity."

She examined the display on his pad, seeing the same readings he was. "What's going on, Rashidi? How are the lights working, or the doors?"

"Or life support," he added.

Daphne checked the instruments built into her spacesuit's forearm panel. He was right; there was air here. Before she could stop him, Rashidi opened his visor. He breathed deeply and nodded at her. Since he hadn't died and the readings had come from their own equipment, she also unsealed her faceplate.

The Moon smelled of spent gunpowder. It was the dust. It got everywhere, even inside a sealed structure. She'd forgotten that smell.

"Suit sensor was right," said Rashidi. "The atmosphere is breathable."

"In this section. Keep your helmet on. First sign of bad air, seal back up."

"I will, trust me."

Daphne's thoughts turned back to comms. She verified she could still raise the Kestrel. Everything looked fine on that front; the computer instantly responded to her ping. That clinched it. Comms on the Moon worked, comms over larger distances didn't.

Rashidi noticed what she was doing. "You're checking on our ship? You worried about it?"

"Making sure it's ready, in case we need to leave in a hurry." There was another reason, but Rashidi wasn't cleared for that, either.

She considered what to do next. Not being able to speak with Ground was frustrating. Well, she was trained to use her initiative. "We have two priorities. I need you to make certain the reactor's offline. I know we're not detecting current in this section, but all these systems have to be powered by something. If electricity's being rerouted, then someone laid new cables. And that someone will be coordinating their activities from the most logical part of the base – Main Mission. I'll investigate whether anything's been disturbed there."

"We're splitting up?"

"The clock is ticking. We have a limited oxygen supply. Besides, there's no reason not to. We're armed. We're familiar with the terrain."

Rashidi snorted. "I was familiar with it over a decade ago."

"It hasn't changed. Remember what we practiced. You see anyone else here, call me. We'll tackle them together."

Rashidi gave a half-assed salute. It was an ironic gesture. Unlike Daphne, he didn't have a military background. He'd been a civilian contractor back in the days of lunar colonization. "You don't want me to shoot on sight?"

"No, Rashidi. Your weapons competency is borderline at best and I want to question whoever's behind this. We handle this carefully and deliberately." The engineer wasn't here for his ability to fight. He was here because he knew how the place worked.

She saw him stiffen, reacting to something behind her. Daphne turned, reaching for her gun.

There was nothing except more white plastic furniture.

"I saw a figure."

"What kind of figure?" she asked. It seemed unlikely a stranger was lurking in this waiting area; there weren't any hiding places. The plaza was a rectangle stretching from the ramp they'd descended to the closed entrance to the base's transit network. No corners or pillars to lurk behind.

"Wearing one of the old uniforms," blurted Rashidi. "A woman. Her face…"

"What about her face?"

Rashidi stammered, "Her skin, it was tinged blue. I saw that once, years ago. Air filtration unit failed in a living module, including the monitoring sensor that should've triggered an alarm. The people didn't realize until it was too late. They suffocated. We opened the doors when they didn't report to work the next day, found them collapsed on the floor. Six dead. I'll never forget."

Daphne had heard about incidents like that. Malfunctions that were one in a million, and still seemed to happen every few months. They didn't normally kill, but every now and then disaster struck.

The high death rate was one of the reasons used to justify never returning to space. One of the talking points trotted out to defend the decision every time people asked why there was an embargo against manned missions.

"There's no one there," she stated.

"I can't explain it. She faded away."

Daphne let out a breath. "I need you to be copacetic, Specialist Onyilogwu." Calling him by rank was rare for her; he preferred being addressed by his first name and she usually went along with that because he wasn't from the services. She did it now to underscore how serious she was. When he addressed her, of course, he used 'commander' or 'Commander Guillory' at her insistence; it was what she was accustomed to. "We're under a lot of stress, I get it. But you can't flake out on me. I can't do this alone."

His jaw clenched. "You won't have to, commander. I'm fine. It must have been a trick of the light." Sweat glistened on the black skin of his face.

"Yeah?"

Rashidi nodded. Daphne wasn't fooled. She could see it in his eyes. The engineer was convinced he'd seen something. "Come on, let's see if the transit tube is functional. Better hope it is, or we're both going to have long walks ahead of us."

***

"Your turn," said Daphne.

Rashidi looked blankly at her.

"For an embarrassing childhood story."

"Oh." He shifted on the long bench seat. Deep humming reverberated throughout the white cabin as the bullet-shaped single-carriage mag-lev train continued its rapid journey along the underground tunnel. Like everything else in the base, the transit system was working just fine without a watt of power. "My formative years were nowhere near as interesting as yours."

They had a minute or two before reaching the base's power plant. She wasn't letting him off the hook so easily.

"You must have one cringeworthy moment that haunts you to this day."

He answered after a pause, "There was one time. I grew up in Nairobi. My elementary school there was middle class. Nothing special but not the worst either. One day, our home room teacher asked us what we wanted to do when we grew up. Standard sort of question, yes? Well, the others, they answered as you'd expect. One girl wanted to be a vet, another a doctor. The boys wanted to be soldiers or fishermen or lawyers. My time to answer came. I told them the truth. I wanted to work in space."

"How did they react?"

He made a dismissive gesture. "They were confused. The teacher asked if I meant I wanted to be an astronaut. Because, you know, Kenya only had a small space program, so that was going to be a challenging career choice. I said no, I didn't want to fly rockets like you saw on the TV, I wanted to go to other worlds and build things. Make towns there for people to live and work in. Get my hands into the soil of planets that people had never touched before. Leave my mark in the night sky."

Daphne could imagine a tiny Rashidi saying that.

The broad-shouldered engineer went on. "How they mocked me. They called me Space Boy for months after that."

"You did, though. Work in space."

He chuckled. "Yes. Thanks to the moonbases taking on contractors from many countries. On my first tour of duty on a moonbase, I did a live call to my old school, answered questions from the kids. They treated me like a star. But, as you know, all that came to an end."

"Yes."

"I never understood why."

Of course you don't, she thought. *The public reasons were always unconvincing, and the secret reason shared with me just a couple of days ago is even harder to swallow.* Out loud, she said, "Too costly. Not enough return on investment. A waste of resources needed on a world combating disease and hunger."

"I suppose so."

She remembered the day she'd learned all space flights were canceled. She'd been back in Louisiana on leave. The news had been devastating.

The train slowed and then halted. Twin sets of doors slid open: one set in the wall of the transit capsule, the other in the wall of the power plant. As with the Kestrel, the double doors formed an airtight seal. The tunnels were too large and leaked too much to pressurize. In most regards, the trains were small, high-speed spacecraft, albeit ones that traveled beneath the lunar surface.

Daphne and Rashidi hopped over to the carriage's exit, their long jumps swallowing the distance. Unlike the first humans to visit the Moon, they were wearing spacesuits that allowed them to move their legs properly, which meant they didn't need to engage in that clumsy Moonwalking gait of Apollo astronauts. Nonetheless, an occasional hop in gravity one-sixth that of Earth's was efficient, not to mention fun.

The power-generating area was deserted, unsurprisingly. Again, the lights were on. There were bare patches on the walls where equipment had been removed during the base's phased closure. Wires trailed out of exposed openings. It was very quiet.

"Your stop, I believe, Space Boy."

Rashidi laughed. "Indeed it is, Reenactment Girl." He stepped out of the train.

"I'll call you for an update in five minutes. I should be in Main Mission by then."

"Very good, commander. I shall be poking at the reactor. Let me know if you stumble across any unauthorized sightseers."

"Right." She waved as the doors closed. There had to be intruders—there was no other explanation. On the other hand, how had they funded, developed, and fully assembled a space program with no one noticing, and how had they mounted an actual launch without being detected? Their own Kestrel's takeoff had required a cover story and the cooperation of several major governments to allay the suspicions of a watchful free press.

She didn't understand what was going on. Neither did her superiors.

The carriage thrummed as it picked up speed.

Perhaps her examination of the base's command center would shed light on the mystery. Distracted, she almost fell as the train lurched.

Shock raced through her. Transit tubes shouldn't shake like that. They were designed to move smoothly so as not send their occupants hurtling into the cabin's walls in the low gravity. Something was wrong.

The tone of the train's hum was altering. It was higher pitched now. The carriage was accelerating. The lights changed to red and a calm voice declared, "Transit tube is exceeding maximum safe speed. Please stand by."

What was doing the talking—the base computer? That couldn't be right. The mainframe computer had been removed.

The rattling of the carriage intensified. Daphne's eyes flicked up to the route map above the doors. The simple display showed a long, flattened loop with symbols for the stops. Each stop lit up as the train passed. The stations were lighting up faster and faster as the train reached an insane velocity.

"Please stand by," repeated the computerized voice. "The speed regulator has malfunctioned."

According to the map, the train was approaching the end of a straight run, where the line turned a tight bend and went back the way it had come. The speed it was going to take that bend, the train was certain to overload the magnetic fields that kept it from scraping against the tunnel wall. It would make physical contact with the lunar rock. The second that happened, the train would catch on the rough surface and be thrown completely off its tracks, twisting sideways in the confined space, both ends smashing simultaneously into the hollowed-out cylinder of the tunnel. The train would disintegrate.

Again, the computer spoke. "Please stand by. This train will terminate at the next station. The next stop is Death. Please stand clear of the doors."

An ear-splitting screech filled the cabin. Daphne threw herself into the nearest seat and tightened the straps of its emergency harness.

The train flipped upside down just as she slammed her helmet visor shut.

***

It was pitch black and Daphne's shoulder hurt. Also, unless she had completely lost her grip on reality, she was hanging from what was now the ceiling.

She tried to make sense of the last few seconds. The terrible shrieking, the wrenching sensation, the sudden plunge into darkness. Before that, the inexplicable announcement from the central computer. The computer that didn't exist. It couldn't have spoken; it was literally impossible. Rashidi wasn't the only person imagining things.

The crash was real, though. So was the pain she was experiencing.

Daphne had to see what condition the train was in before unclipping her seat harness. For all she knew, the section of cabin her seat was bolted to had been torn clear of the rest of the carriage and was wedged into a freshly hewn gouge in the tunnel roof. She could only guess what she'd be falling onto the second she unclipped her restraints—twisted wreckage, bare rock, something liable to damage her suit at any rate. This was not an outcome she wanted, given she was now most likely in a near-vacuum.

She fumbled for her flashlight's controls on her forearm panel. The darkness, at least, was something she could fix.

There were cameras built into her suit's shoulder units as well as lights. By illuminating her surroundings she'd also be providing a better record of events to posterity. Once she restored communications with Ground, they'd want a comprehensible account of what she'd found in Moonbase Gamma, not a lot of blacked-out video. She was planning to be around to tell them in person, of course, but her plans weren't going well so far. The base was old, stripped bare; she'd been told to expect problems with its remaining systems. Finding so much of it in working order, she'd been lulled into a false sense of security. Stupid of her. She'd been picked for her experience. She needed to start using it.

It was hard to find the right suit control in the utter darkness. Her fingers occupied with feeling for the correct toggle, her mind turned to Rashidi. She should call him; let him know what had happened. If she couldn't get herself out of this, she'd need his help. She didn't think she was badly injured, but she could be horribly wrong—it wasn't as if she'd tried moving yet.

At last, her fingertips found the control. Yellowish light spilled out, revealing her surroundings.

Corpses were piled below her. Faces frozen in mid-scream stared up, bodies were strewn in grotesque heaps across broken, sheared-off chairs, limbs lay at impossible angles. Daphne flinched instinctively, before forcing herself to view the scene with scientific detachment. These were moonbase personnel. They wore the distinctive uniforms.

Blood was darkening the tunic of the body directly below Daphne, spreading across its chest. Her eyes flickered to other corpses near her in the mangled carriage. Their wounds, too, were fresh, still bleeding.

Unable to process what she was seeing, Daphne glanced at the far end of the upturned cabin. The flat wall of the cylindrical carriage was crushed, pushed inward by some incredible force. A faint memory came to her, of a transit tube accident more than twenty years ago.

The moonbases had grown larger and larger with each new iteration, necessitating travel networks of increasing complexity. Gamma's underground subway system had required multiple lines, and they crisscrossed, much as terrestrial ones did. Due to cost cutting or poor design, this pinnacle of overcomplication had resulted in the worst lunar disaster in history: two full trains colliding at top speed. Those that hadn't died of their injuries had perished from asphyxiation as the cabins' air had vented into the tunnel.

How could she be seeing this? It was no result of head trauma from her own train crash; the details were too exact. Blood was continuing to seep from torn flesh. The liquid was black in the light cast by her suit. It dripped onto the curve of the cabin's upended roof, forming pools of gore. Steadily, the level of the viscous fluid rose, flooding over the fractured body parts of the corpses at the base of the mound of the dead.

"Rashidi," she called over comms. Her voice was hoarse. "Respond."

Hissing stabbed at her ears. More static, just like the interference that blocked contact with Earth. No, there was a difference, she realized. This time, there was an additional quality to the white noise. Almost the tone of a human voice, or many voices, perhaps. She strained to make out just what the sounds were.

"Look for the dead," she'd been told in the pre-flight briefing. "In space, the dead do not stay in the grave." Ridiculous. It couldn't be true. "We need to know what they're doing."

The rising tide of blood snapped her attention back to the impossible sight beneath her. Already, the vile waters were swamping the middle part of the corpse-hill, and they showed no sign of slowing. What could she do? If she released her harness and dropped, she'd have to wade through the thick fluid while looking for a way out. On the other hand, if she stayed put, the blood would reach her soon enough anyway.

The sheer quantity of blood froze her heart, halted her breathing. There wasn't enough blood in a hundred bodies to fill the cabin, and yet here it was, a lake of death swelling with remorseless intent. Of all the physical impossibilities she'd witnessed since landing here, this was the hardest for her to confront. She could draw her gun—but shooting this slowly churning mass was hardly a solution.

Amidst the static, words clawed their way into audibility. Many voices speaking as one. "We bathed this soil."

"What?" Her response was a gasp.

"We bathed this soil in our blood."

The ichor poured into the compartment with ever greater ferocity. It reached Daphne's dangling boots, coating the orange toecaps. She lifted her feet, not wanting to come into contact with the foul floodwaters. They were evil, malignant; they would contaminate her, breach her suit, invade her flesh. She cast aside any notion of swimming in that coagulation of horror.

"Rashidi!" she called, closer to a scream than she wanted. "Respond, damn it!"

"We bathed this soil with our lifeblood!" roared the voices, blotting out all thought.

Daphne couldn't raise her legs any higher. The blood was going to reach her. She'd be submerged in moments.

She closed her eyes and clenched her teeth so hard it hurt.

Her heart pounded. The sound throbbed through her body.

She felt nothing, not even the uncomfortable pressure of being strapped into a capsized chair.

The eerie voices were gone. So was the static hiss.

"Commander, was that you?" asked Rashidi over the radio. "Are you at Main Mission?"

Daphne opened her eyes.

She was right-side up, in a brightly lit train carriage. In a brightly lit, undamaged carriage, sitting in front of wide-open doors. She was looking out into the cavernous expanse of the empty control center.

The perfectly intact transit capsule had stopped.

***

The silence was eerie.

"Commander Guillory? Are you okay?" Rashidi sounded concerned.

She released the safety harness and stood up. Her legs quivered. "I'm fine. Freaked out, but fine."

"Did something happen?"

"I—" Her mouth worked but refused to make sound. "I don't know. I can't explain it."

"Is anyone there?"

Daphne walked out of the train. She was proud of not running.

The train's double doors led out onto a concourse. From there, a short flight of steps rose to the main part of the chamber. She had a reasonably good view of the entire area without climbing the steps, but she mounted them, nonetheless. Stairs were hardly an inconvenience in low gravity, and she should ensure no one was hiding in the far corners or upper gantries.

"No, it's abandoned. Lifeless." As they'd expected, the mainframe was missing, along with most of the control consoles that had filled the wide floor in years past. Almost everything other than the standard-issue safety warning notices glued to the walls was long-since removed.

"No intruders, then."

"There's nothing here," she confirmed.

"Sorry it's a bust. You'll take the transit system back?"

She blurted, "Christ, no," without meaning to.

Rashidi sounded worried again. "Are you certain you're okay?' He paused, just for a second. "Because I'm not sure I am. This place... it's not right. I keep—"

"Yes?"

"You'll think I'm going crazy, commander."

"Rashidi, I promise you I won't." She was fast reevaluating his story of seeing a woman who'd suffocated to death.

"Well, thing is, I swear I see someone. Not that woman. Not the one that reminded me of... the life support accident. Someone else, this time. A man. I see him out of the corner of my eye. Every time, though, I turn and there's no one there. I know, that's twice I've seen things that aren't there. It's the emptiness of the base, I suppose, it plays tricks. The mind fills in what it expects to be there."

She didn't know about that.

She settled for saying, "I'll take a direct route to you. Find an airlock, walk back to your location across the surface. Look for me knocking on your window."

He laughed.

"I'm serious. When you see me, go check your section's airlock is ready to open from outside."

"Oh, right. That makes sense. What with the airlocks not having been maintained in forever."

Daphne did a cursory sweep of the half-disassembled chamber, mostly to record it was empty for her camera, and then left Main Mission. She followed signs to the nearest airlock.

As it cycled, the pumps sounding wheezy from disuse, she brushed aside a momentary doubt about the integrity of her spacesuit. She hadn't really been in a train accident, after all. Her suit hadn't been put through the mill any more than she had. The crash, the being suspended upside down, the lake of blood—none of that had happened. Except it had, in some way. She was certain of it.

Bounding across the lunar landscape, she felt strangely at peace. The gruesome experience in the transit tube felt far away, and she'd missed walking in the moondust. So long since she'd done this. High in the inky nothingness, Earth gazed down at her. Too far away to make out the continents, but still beautiful. On the horizon, she traced the jagged rim marking the edge of the *lacus* in whose shadow the sprawling base was built. The Lacus Doloris, or the Lake of Sorrow, a basaltic plain more than a hundred kilometers across. To her immediate left lay the outcroppings of the facility's upper story, marking a path for her to follow. On her right, a rugged expanse of dust and regolith stretched away into the gloom.

She hadn't known what to say to Rashidi. Phantasmagoria wasn't included in Space Command's training drills. Perhaps they should have prepped for the world beyond the living as much as environments beyond the terrestrial.

It occurred to Daphne that her spacesuit recorder had been running since they'd arrived on the Moon. She could play back the footage on her forearm display if she wanted. There was no Edit function, to prevent tampering, but Replay was available.

Walking slower so she didn't stumble while distracted, Daphne found the relevant submenu and tapped backward on the time index about ten minutes. That should put her in the train when the weirdness had been in full swing. Her gloved finger hesitated above the Play icon.

What if it showed nothing out of the ordinary? Well, then she would know that the stress of the launch, the mission, the search of the base had gotten to her. She'd put Rashidi in charge—he'd only fantasized individual specters and seemed to be doing better than her—and then report her deteriorating mental state to Ground as soon as contact was reestablished.

The screen jerked into life. Blood filled the display, flowing over the faces of the dead.

"Goddamn!"

"Commander? Is there a problem?"

"No. Turns out I'm not having a psychotic break."

Rashidi said cautiously, "I wasn't aware that was a possibility."

Okay, so she wasn't losing it. Unless she was imagining the footage on her display too. No, that way of thinking *did* lead to insanity.

So, the events in the transit capsule had definitely occurred.

That led to a whole new set of problems. *How* had they happened? What was behind it all?

Her analysis was interrupted by what she saw then in the lee of the power plant's exterior wall.

Row upon row of neat rectangular hillocks in the gray lunar landscape.

She knew what they were. Graves. Hundreds of them.

***

There was nothing supernatural about this sight.

Daphne examined grave after grave, reading the inscriptions on the headstones. Many of them gave the cause of death. Often it was something humdrum: sudden illnesses that struck down the victims before they could be medevacked to Earth. In a lot of other cases, though, the causes were more violent. Kestrel crashes, fuel fires, radiation exposure, catastrophic life support failure, munitions malfunctions... the list was extensive. Near the middle of the memorials was a stone monument to the casualties of the transit accident.

This was the cost of manned exploration, of offworld colonization, the cost in lives. Here it was, laid out in careful lines. Progress, she reflected, was achieved by treading on the bones of the fallen.

Prior to the first settlements being constructed on the Moon, only three astronauts had actually died in space. Sure, many more had given their lives on launch pads, or during ascents, but they—technically—had died on Earth or in the sky above it. It was in 1971 that three cosmonauts died in space proper, above the Kármán line at a hundred kilometers, killed by the accidental depressurization of their Soyuz 11 vehicle as it began atmospheric reentry. They had remained the sole fatalities at those distances until the twenty-second century and lunar expansion. At that point, the death toll had increased rapidly.

Daphne was aware of the sacrifices people had made. She'd never forgotten. She'd never hesitated to put her own life on the line, either. The risks were worth it, as far as she was concerned. The retreat from space had always been difficult for her to stomach. Short-sighted. Foolish. That's what she thought.

Satisfied there was nothing untoward lurking among the cemetery plots, Daphne made her way in long strides to the side of the building where Rashidi was performing his examination of the reactor. She banged on the windows until he noticed her. The Kenyan let her in.

"I have something to tell you," he said as the inner hatch opened.

"Let me get my faceplate up, won't you?"

"The reactor isn't generating power."

She looked at him for several seconds. He appeared to be serious. "Talk me through it, Rashidi. Explain how all these lights and doors and airlocks and trains work with no electricity." They'd asked that question earlier, and Daphne had assumed power had simply been rerouted along new cables by whoever had reactivated the base. The point had lurked, unhappy, in the back of her mind, though, the explanation never sitting well with her.

He guided her to the back of the room and the viewing panel that allowed visual observation of the reactor. There was a large sign over the viewing slit reading 'RADIATION DANGER. ABSOLUTELY NO ADMITTANCE BEYOND THIS POINT. USE ROBOTIC EQUIPMENT FOR ALL OPERATIONS. NO HUMAN PRESENCE PERMITTED INSIDE REACTOR.'

Rashidi gestured through the thick glass of the viewport. "Anything strike you as unusual?" Not being an expert on Uranium-235/Thorium reactors, Daphne didn't know what to look for.

Impatient, Rashidi spun the wheel of the emergency access lock all the way open and then hauled on it. The observation window, it transpired, was part of an enormous metal hatch, several feet thick, that swung out into the room. Daphne was forced to step back.

No alarms blared. They were either disassembled or some minor part had corroded into uselessness—maybe a capacitor on a motherboard had dried out. Electronics left idle for years suffered relatively minor degradation, but it didn't take more than a few vulnerable components here and there to break down to stop an entire system from functioning.

"Is opening that wise?"

"Why? Because of the radiation?" He nodded at the jumble of pipes and metal shapes she assumed was the reactor. "There isn't any. Not enough to worry about, anyway. They didn't just take away the fuel rods like I expected—they stripped out the entire core. Probably buried it in a pit out on the surface. Precautionary measure to stop terrorists getting their hands on unguarded materials for a dirty bomb."

"There couldn't be another reactor somewhere else in the base?" She doubted it but felt obliged to ask.

Rashidi rubbed his eyes through his open visor. "I don't think so, commander. There was only one in the old days. To build a replacement, you'd need to ship in a huge amount of equipment. How could anyone do that without being spotted through telescopes?"

There it was. The base was consuming energy even though it didn't, couldn't, produce any.

Her mind teased at the impossible things she'd seen, experienced. The ghost of a computer had spoken in the train. Was it possible the ghost of a reactor powered the base?

"Rashidi, I have something to tell you, as well. You're not alone in seeing things here that you can't explain. I've seen horrifying visions. More than visions. Stuff that was real, in that moment."

He let out a high-pitched titter; a laugh strangled before it could descend into hysteria. It sounded like a squall of murdered amusement. "What's happening to us? We're veterans of Space Command. We were chosen for this mission because of our ability to stay level-headed in a crisis."

Daphne broke protocols, then. She told Rashidi the Big Secret, even though she'd been ordered not to reveal it to the mission specialist. As far as the bigwigs on the ground were concerned, he didn't need to know. That's how they operated—they kept the truth compartmentalized, handing out just enough for their underlings to be effective. They hadn't wanted to tell her, either. But a commander had to know what she was getting into. If they wanted her to divine the motives of the departed she had to first know they were unquiet.

"The dead don't stay dead on the Moon, Rashidi. They come back." There, she'd done it. Disobeyed orders.

It had taken a lot for her to accept ghosts were possible here. Now, she did. Rashidi needed to believe it too. Or he'd never realize the danger he was in.

He took a step away from her. "I've witnessed inexplicable phenomena here, commander. Things that I don't understand. But that's a little much. We're supposed to be rational people."

"I didn't believe it, either. And when I saw, I doubted the evidence of my own eyes. Even now, there's a part of me that still doubts. We have to face it, though. It's real."

Rashidi scowled. "Ghosts."

"As you say, ghosts."

"The paranormal."

"What we've encountered is outside current scientific understanding. That doesn't mean it won't be explained one day."

"I don't know what you want me to say."

"Rashidi, this is why space agencies only send out robotic probes now. No one knew when we started building here. There was no way of knowing until people started dying out in the cold and the dark. The first people to perish in space, three cosmonauts back in the twentieth century, they died during descent—there was nowhere for them to haunt in the upper atmosphere. But if someone dies here, in this base, they can endure, separated from their flesh. Don't you see? This is the true reason crewed spaceflight was abandoned--*the dead don't stay dead in space.*"

"That's why the bases were evacuated?"

"The reason was kept from us. But, yeah, people started seeing apparitions up here. There were casualties, murders attributed to those manifestations. It took the authorities a long time to figure out what was happening. In the end, they couldn't deny it any longer. It wasn't safe to keep personnel on base. They had to shut everything down. And the governments who ran the bases, they didn't want the reason to get out."

"That there's life after death?"

"No, that we turn into homicidal maniacs when we come back." That was the horror of it: the loss of reason, the plunge into blind rage, a frenzy of hate that lasted forever. The dead wanted to make the living like them. Deceased mothers would seek out their own children and slaughter them without hesitation. No wonder government leaders were afraid how the human race would react to the revelation.

Rashidi raised a hand in objection. "Wait. If ghosts are real, and lunatics, if you'll forgive the term, why aren't they swarming the Earth, wreaking havoc?"

"The way it was laid out to me, on Earth, death is *old*. There's a fog of souls that have ended, too many to ever hear one voice in the chorus. It's a background whisper, always there, part of normal existence. We never notice it. Each new death is a tiny fraction of what has gone before, each spirit dissolves into the soup, all self-awareness dispersed. That's not what happens here. On the Moon—and everywhere else in space—death is new. These places have been sterile for billions of years. Then humans brought life, and death. That death is a fresh wound. The souls have no fog into which they can be absorbed, nothing in which they're diluted down. The result—ghosts purer than anything humanity has ever encountered before. Spirits of intense concentration. Here, the dead can kill."

"If that's true, space is forever lost to us." He shook his head furiously. "No, it's too much. I can't accept it."

"You need proof? They show up on camera. Review the footage from your shoulder cam. That figure you said you keep glimpsing—it'll be somewhere in what you've recorded."

Without a word, Rashidi did as she bid. Minutes passed as he scrolled through clip after clip. He narrowed his search to a short time period after he'd entered the power plant, checking and rechecking segments around that timestamp. Daphne began to despair he'd find anything. Then, he stopped tapping the screen. "There."

She craned her neck and saw what he'd found. At the very edge of the display, blurry but clear enough—a man in the old moonbase uniform. His hair was wild, his eyes glazed, his complexion drained bone white. His hands were stretched out; fingers bent like talons. "I didn't imagine him."

"You didn't." Daphne looked up from the display on Rashidi's forearm unit. The crazed figure stood inches away, on Rashidi's far side, just out of his peripheral vision. Her brain started to form a warning.

Too late. The apparition fell upon Rashidi, grappling with him. Daphne was knocked backward. She stumbled and regained her footing.

The ghost screamed, clawing at her crewmate's suit. Rashidi fought the unliving madman as best he could. The figure was unbelievably strong. It was all Rashidi could do to protect his face. With a crack, a powerful blow shattered the left of Rashidi's unlatched faceplate, causing it to separate from the helmet.

Daphne unholstered her gun.

"Ghosts are attacking us!" shrieked the phantasm, its words disassociated from its frenzied attack. "We've got to get out of here!" It took hold of Rashidi's shoulders.

The outburst made Daphne pause. The ghost thought it was fleeing from ghosts. Was this what it remembered from its final moments of life?

Rashidi wrestled with the figure's grip, unable to tear himself free. Daphne raised her sidearm and fired. The bullet passed clean through the crazed apparition, leaving a ripple in whatever it was made of. She heard the projectile strike the wall.

The figure was pushing Rashidi toward the still-open inner airlock hatch, the one she'd entered through. There was no time to think. Daphne dropped the gun—it was useless anyway—and grabbed at the spectral entity. Her gloved hands did, at least, connect with something tangible; a form the consistency of gelatin. The quasi-solid wraith threw her clear with a shrug.

Rashidi's efforts similarly did no good. He was forced back, back into the airlock, his boots scraping against the slick flooring every inch of the way. "Let go of me," he gasped. The ghost tightened its grip.

"We have to leave!" it moaned. "I'll save you."

The external hatch began to open inward. That violated basic physics. With the interior hatch open as well, the air pressure in the base should have prevented the outer one from moving. A wind whistled past Daphne, growing in strength. She flipped her visor closed, resealing her helmet. Rashidi couldn't do the same; his helmet was damaged. He shouted, "Commander!"

Those were the last words he spoke as a living creature.

The ghost hauled the mission specialist out onto the lunar surface. Rashidi's body thrashed wildly. His suit attempted to preserve pressure in the unsealed helmet, spewing forth its air supply in a vaporizing cloud of gas. Daphne scrambled after the pair. Reaching them, she saw Rashidi was losing consciousness, wrenching at the specter's death grip with weaker and weaker motions. Again, she tried to pry free the ghost's fingers from Rashidi's shoulders. Again, she failed.

The grim battle continued, seconds dragging into a minute, then two minutes. Rashidi's suit exhausted its air reserves. Hopelessness, then dull resignation, seeped into his gaze. His hands fell from the specter, grappling no more, fighting for life no more. Daphne did not falter in her own efforts, meaningless though they were.

If only she could get Rashidi back inside the base. She might yet save his life. But the damned ghost wouldn't let go. In its terror, it was oblivious to what it was doing.

Suddenly, the apparition faded. Daphne was no longer yanking at its arms. She fell backward in slow motion, taking an eternity to hit the dust-strewn ground.

Laying there, staring into the gaping oval where Rashidi's faceplate should have been, she witnessed that ineffable moment when the glint of vitality guttered in his eyes and they became the lusterless orbs of a corpse.

In a final spasm, his fingers dug into the barren grit and, in so doing, took within their grasp soil that no other human had ever touched before or ever would again.

***

"Rashidi's dead." Daphne spoke aloud so her words would be recorded by her spacesuit. Her breath was labored from traversing the landscape. Another four hundred meters to reach the pad where she'd set down in the Kestrel. "I was not able to free him from his attacker in time."

A cold summation of a cold fact. Revealing the truth to him had, ultimately, achieved nothing. Would he have survived if she'd told him earlier? Ground control listened to everything said in the Kestrel. They'd be eavesdropping now if it weren't for the interference. They would have known the second she violated her oath of secrecy. She should have done it anyway. Better to be brought up on charges than for Rashidi to die. Too late for regrets now, though. Now there was only the mission.

"For what it's worth, I agree with mission control's preliminary evaluation of the situation here. The base's reactivation is the result of supernatural activity. I believe the dead are using their own energies to power the facility. They seem able to affect how we perceive it as well, simulating events from the past."

To reach her craft, she had two options: either cover the distance using the corridors of the base and reenter the vehicle via the travel terminal's waiting plaza, or hike across the intervening terrain and gain access to pad eight through its ground-level entrance. Either route afforded entry to the skywalk hooked up to the Kestrel. Daphne chose to limit her time inside the base, going overland for the majority of the distance. Once at the pad, she'd cut through the disused vehicle repair bay underneath the

Kestrel. Less time in the moonbase meant less scope for the ghosts to attack her.

Probably.

"I have not made progress on the secondary priority of determining the ghost's objectives in restoring the base to a semblance of life. Nor do I know why they recreate scenes from the past." She did have an idea of what to do next, though. Trigger the bomb in the Kestrel.

Another aspect of the mission she'd kept from Rashidi. They'd brought a warhead with them. It was hidden in the Kestrel's main compartment.

The decision was simple. Stop the base falling into enemy hands. The dead were the enemy. The bomb wouldn't kill ghosts. It would, however, deny them the facility.

She couldn't guess what they intended. Nothing that benefited the living, that was for sure. The ghosts had tried to kill her in a train crash, they'd murdered Rashidi; they were undeniably hostile. As for *why* they hated the living, perhaps they were consumed by jealousy or spite. Left alone, they could launch an attack on Earth. No wonder Space Command had wasted no time in putting a mission together.

Two hundred meters to the pad now. She was covering the ground quickly, bounding along with huge strides. Reflected light from a base window glinted on metal. Daphne slowed and took in the new sight.

It was the mangled remains of the robotic probe Space Command had dispatched before they'd resorted to a human-led expedition. She'd known the probe had landed close by. That's why the pad had been selected for Daphne's Kestrel, to afford her an opportunity to discover its fate. Here it was, torn to pieces. Another victim of the ghosts' hatred. The outside, it seemed, was every bit as accessible to the departed as the base.

That insight kept her going.

Tiredness nipped at her muscles as she arrived at the tall wall of metal that formed the side of the landing pad. The Kestrel was at the top of the pad, just a few meters away. One-sixth Earth gravity meant the highest Daphne could jump was about three meters. Since the pad's surface was over four meters straight up and there were no handholds, its proximity was nothing more than a tease. She needed to get back inside the moonbase.

The first airlock she tried wouldn't budge, the mechanism seized from long years of neglect. The second entry point responded, to her relief.

The base was not as she'd left it. The cavernous hangar bay was unlit and unheated. As her shoulder lights flicked on, she could feel the tomb-like cold seeping through the material of her spacesuit. Its heating filaments auto-adjusted to a higher setting to compensate. Thank God she checked the environmental readings before unlatching her faceplate. There was no atmosphere inside this section.

The base was insulated. Much of it was underground, including more than half of the hangar she was in. Warmth from the other sections should have bled through here. Even assuming this particular chamber's environmental systems had not been reactivated, it should not have been this frigid in the empty repair bay. It couldn't have got this cold so quickly.

Unless the rest of the base had never been thawed out in the first place. It occurred to her that if the heating hadn't been real then the other aspects of life support might not have been, either. There might not be an atmosphere anywhere in the base. Maybe there never had been. Ghosts didn't need warmth or air.

She and Rashidi hadn't imagined the air, though. Her suit's sensors had measured it; she'd breathed it. Equally, her suit had videoed a lake of blood filling a transit capsule's interior. The dead decided what was real in their domain, and when it existed at all.

Putting aside the unsettling notion that she'd been walking around a base, helmet wide open, sucking in lungsful of air that didn't exist, Daphne closed the airlock behind her and proceeded along the gantry. The metal walkway encircled the hangar's interior wall about halfway up, affording Daphne a view of the entire chamber, or as much of it as her suit's lights could illuminate. Cranes hung in the shadows overhead, and empty parts and service trenches dotted the perimeter floor with rectangles of impenetrable black. Obscure tangles of machinery squatted near them in the gloom—refueling pumps, she guessed. In the center stood a massive hydraulic lift, extended all the way to the ceiling. If the lift could have been trusted, Daphne would have used it to lower the entire pad down into the maintenance area, bringing the ship to her. Better not to touch the mechanism, though. She'd climb down a ladder to the gray concrete floor and use the interior accessway to get to the lounge area. Then up the ramp and across the skywalk to her Kestrel. A more circuitous route but she didn't have much choice.

She began to clamber down the ladder.

The hangar transformed. Light filled the echoing metal cavern. The cranes held Kestrels in their clamps, taking them to designated service trenches. Technicians moved below her. Ghosts tending phantom ships.

Another spectral tableau. She knew in her gut it would culminate in some catastrophe. She didn't want to be caught halfway down a ladder when that happened. Placing her boots on the outside of the ladder's rails and loosening her grip slightly, Daphne allowed herself to slide down the final meter. Then she ran for the doorway that led away from the hangar.

She was almost at the hatchway when the Kestrel fell from the crane. She watched it fall, saw it strike a fuel pump. An explosion bloomed, consuming the hangar. Kestrel after Kestrel detonated, men and machines were incinerated. A wall of flame roared into her. She shielded her faceplate with her gloves and screamed five words.

"I know what you want!"

The flames vanished.

***

"It took me a while," Daphne confessed. "But I get it now. You were reenacting the past. I should have understood sooner. I used to do that. I reenacted the past. Brought it back to life. Not to endlessly re-live events for some vicarious thrill, not to dwell on historical pain, but so that others could learn from it. So they could feel it, comprehend it at a gut level. That's why you showed me the train crash. The accident in the hangar. That's why you showed Rashidi the woman who died of suffocation.

You wanted us to know, you even said it as plain as you could—you bathed this soil with your blood."

Her escort did not speak. She got the impression they were listening.

Lines of silent shimmering figures walked on either side of her. Each of the phantasms wore their wounds with careless dignity. They did not hide how they had died.

Sore from the unreal explosion, Daphne rode in a six-wheeled lunar buggy. Its battery had died years before, but the wraiths kept it going. The ghosts kept pace with the vehicle effortlessly. They left no footsteps in the dust; she doubted their feet interacted with the ground in any way she'd understand.

She could guess their destination: the cemetery. They wanted every spirit on the Moon to hear. All had sacrificed equally, all deserved equal measure of justice.

In the lee of the abandoned power plant, she saw the rows of graves. Bodies hauled themselves clear of the sterile dirt and stood before her in stern ranks. It was a parliament of spirit corpses.

Rashidi was with them.

"Did you need to kill him?" she asked, gesturing toward the specialist. "I know, you were showing me what happened. The way the living reacted to encountering the dead. The panic, the fear. The blind urge to run, how terror overcame reason." She fought back tears. "We only knew each other a short time, but he was my friend." She wondered how much the ghosts could control their own actions. How much they could overcome their own instincts. They, too, were human.

What would a diplomat say in a situation like this? 'Mistakes have been made on both sides?' She felt like an ambassador. A delegate sent to represent the living.

The apparitions stirred. They were growing restless.

"You're right to be angry." She held up her hands in a gesture of peace. "You're right. You gave your lives in the cause of conquering the infinite, and those sacrifices shouldn't be for nothing. You want the blood you spilled to count for something, to mean something for the future.

You want people to return to the Moon, to continue the work you started. So there's a point to all the suffering."

She stared into their sad eyes. "I'll tell the people back on Earth. I'll make them understand. I will speak for the dead."

She wasn't going to detonate her warhead. The base would be needed by the colonists to come.

***

"I'm glad I get to spend more time with you," Daphne said, glancing at Rashidi. The ghost cycled through familiar motions—checking and rechecking the screens in the Kestrel's cockpit. Reenacting the past.

She watched him for a while. The craft had left lunar orbit and there weren't any course adjustments to make for several more hours.

"You must have something embarrassing in your past," he asked. "Something you cringe at the thought of, even now."

The radio hissed into life. It was ground control, finally able to reach them now they were far enough from the moonbase and its population of spirits.

"Hold that thought," she said to her crewmate, suspecting he wouldn't have much choice.

Static cut through every third word received over comms. Daphne knew it was the energy pouring off Rashidi to blame.

"I hope you can hear me clearly, Ground. This is Commander Guillory. You should be getting the telemetry and audio-visual recordings from the mission now—all the footage we couldn't transmit live. It's a lot of data for you to go through, but I think you should review it. I'll give you a moment or two. Remember, it's locked at our end, no Edit feature enabled. Everything you'll see is real."

The response was garbled. It sounded like they were indeed checking the data.

She waited. Seeing Rashidi next to her in the Kestrel would cause considerable confusion, she had no doubt, when they viewed the part where he died.

She wondered how long his ghost could remain intact. The closer they got to Earth, the more his spectral form would get caught up in the powerful sea of souls that saturated her world. She thought it unlikely Rashidi's spirit could survive exposure closer than the Van Allen belts. At that range she anticipated he'd disperse. That gave her two more days with him. She'd take it.

The ghost had insisted on accompanying her. Maybe he didn't fully understand what would happen. Maybe he didn't care.

Enough time had passed, she felt. She reopened comms. "As you know now, we lost Mission Specialist Onyilogwu. The cost of this voyage was high. Nevertheless, as I'm sure he'd tell you himself, we did find the answers we were sent to find. The probe was destroyed, and the base was reactivated, because the people we left behind wanted humanity to return. Those acts were an invitation. No, more than that, they were a demand. A demand that the human race not give up, not run away in ignorance and fear."

"Commander Guillory," stuttered the radio. "Are you confirming the base is in the hands of the, er, forces we predicted?"

How coy they were. They were frightened of being heard by the billions they'd lied to. She was sick of secrets.

"You were wrong, thirteen years ago. The dead reached out to us. They were clumsy, and confused, and they weren't sure how to do it. I get why your response was to pull back. It must have been chaotic when the ghosts manifested in large numbers. But when we left, they realized something—something you missed. Without us, their deaths lost all purpose. Without us, there was no one to remember them."

The radio hissed again. "What is the meaning of this?"

"I'll tell you what this means. Tell the generals and politicians there at mission control too. The dead are not the enemy. They travel with us. We carry them with us in our hearts. The dead are us. We should not fear them, no more than we should fear ourselves. It is only by understanding them that we can move forward. They want us to move forward, to the Moon and then the stars. Even though, in the end, it will destroy them."

"Destroy them?"

She glanced at Rashidi and answered the mission controller's question. "Sure. Ghosts can't endure on Earth because too many deaths have accumulated. The spirit field has grown so strong it tears them apart. If we live in space long enough, that effect will build again, in each place where humans dwell. The dead can only visit us for a short while, and to see them anew we'll need to spread ever onward to new worlds. We can have an afterlife—one we can touch and measure. The cost is that we abandon our fear and quest for the stars, leaving our mark on infinity. Are you ready for the challenge?"

By her side, Rashidi rechecked the displays in endless repetition. This time, though, there was a smile on his lips.

Where the Monsters Are

By Mike Morgan

Malcolm Tensor was a spy for the British government--one of the best. Sixteen years after wild magic was unleashed on an unsuspecting world and monsters stalk every corner of the globe, he's the leader of a Kill-or-Contain squad. His mission: to scour the north of the UK for unregistered magical creatures and... take care of them by whatever means necessary. He, too, was transformed by the explosion of magic so long ago, but he's still a patriot, and he knows his duty. When terrorists strike at the heart of the new order, Tensor is astonished to find his team reassigned to normal duties. Why is he being sidelined? Why does the government need so many monsters rounded up? Tensor won't stop until he finds the answers, no matter the cost. There is evil lurking beneath the center of London... evil older than anything he can imagine...

https://www.hiraethsffh.com/product-page/where-the-monsters-are-by-mike-morgan

Solitary Potter's Field
Margarida Brei

Potter's Field is a lonely sad place,
Where the dead find no rest.
No elaborate mausoleums,
no marble or intricate work,
Just a plain ugliness and a doleful clerk.

The graveyard is barren
The rumour is at night the ferryman of
Hades tries to carry the dead souls away.
The psychopomp hates Potter's Field,
There most souls against his carrying off are sealed.

Potter's Field where the unclaimed
or indigent are buried,
Akeldama or field of blood
is a place foul and harried.
No one visits, no one cares,
No one cries or their hair tears.

The grass is long and shaggy,
The shadows are sad, scraggy and saggy.
At night lost souls flit about,
Society has blanked them out.

The Galvanic
James Dorr

"Ye may say that bankers have hearts of flint," Dr. N_____ proclaimed -- I will not say what his name was here, though you would recognize it if you saw it -- "or likewise men of the legal professions, but I will tell you that there are none so hard and unyielding as those of our own Edinburgh physicians."

We strained to hear him, my fellow neophytes and I, as we waited in the dimly lit chamber above Surgeons' Hall for what was to be our first full-body anatomy session. The gas jets' hiss vied with his words for our instructor was quite into his years, so old in fact that he himself had studied under the notorious Dr. Knox, and, prior to that, both Drs. Monro, *secundus et tertius*. His voice thus could rise to little more than a whisper, but he whose work on *The Branchings of the Human Nerve System* is still read today, continued to perform demonstrations as his health permitted. And even when not he remained with the College, as he did this night, if not to deliver the lecture from the platform behind the cadaver himself, then at least to wield the exemplary pointer.

Oh, his hands were still steady, if his voice was not -- more steady that night than those of some of our own young students, I would dare say myself. One of our fellows had already fainted, in anticipation, and more than one looked a bit green at the jowls. But the old man went on.

"Let me tell you," he said, "of the corpse you will be seeing cut open soon. But before even that, let me tell you a story. . . ."

***

In days some time back (the aged surgeon said), before the Warburton Anatomy Act was finally passed in '32 which thus allowed subjects for lectures as this night's to be come by legally, there were men -- often of dubious honesty -- who had to be dealt with, known variously as

"Resurrectionists" or "Sack-'em-up Men." These were the ones who supplied the bodies for Schools such as this one, as well as the various private lectures most physicians offered.

The money was good, you see, for their labors. Cadavers were needed -- they had to be gotten -- and therefore could command prices of thirty or forty pounds or more to those that dug them up. More than enough to provide a living for men with little of education and still less of morals, even when out of the take would come bribes for churchyard sextons, and guards and others, to find different places to cast their eye when the digging and sacking were going on.

So it was too, though, that some cut corners -- the Burkes and Hares of our fair city, the Bishops and Mays of London, and others -- and some of the corpses received were, to put a delicate point to it, overly fresh. And others were stolen from fellow Sack-'em-ups, often from Ireland and shipped to our own shores. Gangs roamed the streets for that, robbers of robbers, and not averse to "Burking" their own fellows should the opportunity come for it, requiring only that first there be liquor sufficient to quiet the intended victim in order that the corpse be procured without marks of violence.

Oh, those were shameful days, made all the worse by the rivalries among our own physicians -- stealing students one from the other to increase their own fees as well as their learning. But as one's number of students grew larger, so too did the need for more bodies in order to support yet more lectures. And so the cycle grew, feeding upon itself. Corpses were often mailed in from the countryside by rural constables, seeking to turn a profit from other people's misfortunes. Bodies from hospitals sometimes were "mislaid" before they could be claimed by grieving relations. And we, the physicians, the doctors and students, did nothing to stop this. We *needed* cadavers. One cannot bring an ill person to health unless one has first learned the body's workings, how flesh and muscle and bone and sinew are put together, how nerves and blood vessels bring spark and nutrition to all fleshly parts, that the whole might enjoy life. And thus we, life's saviors or so we would hope to be, given enough learning and enough skill, contributed most in our own at-all-costs-avoid-questioning-too-deeply-whence-subjects-came way to what had become the mockery of death's peace.

And then, Burke and Hare. As I said before, though others preceded them, the need for bodies became so great that some did not even go to the churchyard, but rather selected the poor, the friendless, the widowed, the lonely, the all-but-forgotten shadows of humankind, lost in its corners -- or so they thought! -- and did them in on the very streets! And all for the rapaciousness of we, the doctors.

Of course they were needed. The bodies, that is. Science could not advance without them, both for demonstrations for learning, and for other matters. And so too were the Sack-'em-ups needed in increasing numbers, the latter of course to supply of the former.

But when the ghastly art turned to murder . . . ah, that's when the outcry went up of "foul!" Bad enough to rob graves, and now the public had roused itself up against the ghouls. And against the ghouls' employers as well.

Knox, who in innocence had but received a fresh-murdered body, found his career ruined. His house nearly burned down. And yet, for us others, by now there was no stopping receiving corpses, whatever their provenance, lest their suppliers should peach on *us* and we be ruined too.

Thus was the winter of 1830, a year after Burke's hanging and, by the irony of the law at that time, anatomizing by Monro *tertius* in public session as warning to others who might perform murder. I had of course left Dr. Knox by then -- to have done otherwise would have been unsafe -- sojourning on the Continent some while with Prof. F____ and Dr. T____. And so, when I returned to Scotland intending to start my own surgical practice, I found conditions somewhat changed.

Oh, the old rivalries among physicians still continued, if anything fiercer than when I had left, but the Resurrectionists' ways had evolved as they, too, had been forced to take a lower profile. Needing cadavers, I found an Irishman who could provide them. But as that winter proceeded on to spring, all of a sudden, as these things would happen from time to time, the supply dwindled.

I could not find other Sack-'em-up Men to augment this supply without incurring the wrath of the man I was already in with. Such was the power these men had over us -- blackmailers, really, as they turned out to be -- that it was almost as if we did *their* bidding than they did ours. And so my Irishman, when I accosted him about the necessity of getting new corpses, put this somewhat peculiar proposition to me:

"Guv'nor," he said, "I do have this one body, and it shall be yours as soon as it's ready. And I can get others on similar terms. But ye must pay first. Ye get me drift on this?"

I shook my head. "No." I did not get his drift, yet.

He explained himself further. "The body is *mine*. As ye see, I'm in ill health -- I shan't have much time left in any event so I may as well spend me last months in comfort." He coughed as if to underscore his point, but I believed him. The work at night. The digging of corpses, some that had passed away of diseases. Not to mention the wrath of the mob that still persisted, making it dangerous for one to be seen on the city's streets at night with just so much as a pick or a shovel. All these conspired to make Resurrection work, at the least, an unhealthy trade.

"But," I protested, "I need a cadaver now. Whether yours or not -- and, yes, I see now your hand's palsied shaking and have no doubt of its readiness soon -- it must be in my chambers by tomorrow."

"Yes," said my Irishman. "I understand that. But, as I grow frail in my labor, so too has my sister who, as luck would have it, passed on just this evening. She had no friends, Guv'nor. I've told no one of it. And so I suggest to ye that if ye buy my corse on promise, to use as it's ready, I'll sell ye hers also."

What choice had I then? To buy an option on this man's own corpse struck me as foolish. Should he renege later, what recourse would there be? Surely not that of law! And, as I discovered the following winter when, as if by a miracle, his health had come back sufficiently for him to force me to buy a renewal on it, I was more than foolish.

And yet, whether it be that of his sister, or of some poor streetwalker he'd had his eye on intending a Burking, I did need a body. And I needed it quickly.

And so, God help me, I took up his offer.

***

Dr. N_____ paused then and signaled one of us to bring him down a pitcher of water. While we waited, I thought I could hear the creak of a door downstairs, and then a faint whirring. The opening, possibly, of a back entrance to the hall, as well, who knows?, as the buzz of flies maybe. The night was quite warm and even though, under the present law, paupers' bodies could be got from hospitals provided no relatives stood in objection -- and that they be given good Christian burial when they were done with -- sometimes they would still not be quite of the freshest. And then the faint sound of a gasp -- a shriek, maybe.

But by then Dr. N_____ had received his water and, confirming that the lecture would indeed be starting shortly, he placed the emptied glass back on its tray and continued his story.

***

Was this Irishman a Burker? A murderer as well as a robber of churchyards? I have little doubt he was. You see, among doctors, though rivals we were, it was quite difficult for such things to be kept a secret. Our rivalry itself was the cause -- we eagerly stole students from one another, passing them back and forth just as first one, then another of us would gain reputation for some new technique or experimentation. And so I had my share of others' students, as they had of mine, and these students brought gossip. Including gossip about this man who supplied to others as well as to me.

But that does not matter, concerning my story. What does is this: That my Irishman had become too greedy. I heard the gossip and soon ascertained that I was not the only surgeon who had paid him well, and continued to pay, for the promise of the use of his own body.

And so I called truce among us surgeons, discussing this, my new found knowledge, first with Dr. B_____ the Elder, then with the others, and confirmed that all, or nearly all, of the prominent surgeons of Edinburgh had paid this man for his corpse after death. Indeed, some had paid him for many years for it.

Now when our meeting occurred was in late spring, and then, as now, the Schools closed down from May to October. Thus we determined a confrontation, having no fear of repercussion -- at least in terms of his refusing to supply us further should we press him too far -- in that we still should have plenty of time to find new sources for the next session. We queried our students and, sure enough, there were several who had an idea of where our man resided. And so one evening the first week of May we marched to the poorer section of town, a fair mob ourselves of torch-bearing doctors, to have it out with him.

What we would have done with him I do not know, except he was forewarned and, seeing our approach from his windows, determined to flee. He lit out a back gate of his tenement and, with us nearly upon his heels, coursed down winding streets and cobble-stoned alleys, often in darkness or nearly in darkness. So the pursuit went, a mile or more, with all the time a fog starting to rise up out of the Firth, when, all of a sudden, he dodged out into the lights of a wide square and directly into the path of a carriage.

The driver pulled his horses up as best he could, but already it was too late to avoid him. We, as doctors, of course took the body that even though most terribly trampled, still had some spark of life left within it. We took him to Surgeons' Square and to this very building here and, such was our oath, we did the best we knew how to save him. To save his worthless life which before -- who knows what we might have done in our anger? And yet. . .

***

Dr. N_____ paused again to take more water. His voice had been failing, and yet we'd been listening with such rapt attention I doubt a one of us had missed a single word. In the silence we heard the gas jets and, underneath, in the hall below, the sounds of rustling. Of surgical instruments being made ready. A soft keening sound like the grunt of a workman, perhaps in his straining to move the table the subject of the night would be laid on.

And then, the strength of his voice renewed somewhat, the old man continued.

***

God help me, I say. We are all of us God-fearing men in this room, I think. Learning the wonder of God's creation, the image of God laid out in Man's body, despite what some of the Rationalists say can only serve to strengthen our Faith, not to cause it to falter. And yet, as we struggled to save this poor man's life, despite the grievance we justly had of him, I saw the looks of my fellow doctors. I saw how they glanced as the spark of life faded, then finally snuffed out, as if it were pity his corpse had been trampled and so, unless the tedious work of repairing its damage be somehow accomplished before it go bad, was of no use to them.

And, moreover, it was nearly summer. . . .

At last first one, and then another, gave up the task. Dr. M_____ signed the death certificate, then singly and in pairs they departed, some of them murmuring that, at the end, the Irishman had at least saved them the problem of which, of the many he had sold himself to, would be able to lay claim upon him.

But I, I had studied in France as I say, and also Vienna. I had studied under T_____ and F_____ who, in their own turn, had been disciples of the celebrated Franz Anton Mesmer. I had a grounding, rare for a Scottish surgeon at that time, in the theories of Galvani, that animal life was the cause of electromagnetic force, and of their refutation by Volta. And I had, myself, formulated my own thoughts.

Thus, alone with this newly-dead subject, unable to save him by other means, I now determined to try these out. I called for servants, had them bring me Voltaic cells, a large tub of water, and salts and powders and coils of copper wire. Into the tub I placed the Irishman, fixing the coils to his hands and feet, and started the current.

I fully expected his feet to kick, as Galvani's frogs' legs did, a mere reaction as Volta had proved to the force that flowed into them from the charged cells. But I also expected, as Mesmer had, that there might be more to it, that Volta as well had not seen the whole picture. And so I proved that night.

I never did publish the whole that I learned. And that for good reason. But Volta was wrong in not following up his work's conclusions. That, yes, it was true that animal life was not the creator of electrical forces, but -- and this he failed to see -- quite the opposite thing *was* the case. That Galvani, after all, had been the farther along the correct track.

That, properly applied to a subject, electrical force was the cause of life.

***

"But why?" one of we students interrupted as our aged instructor once more briefly paused. "That is, you say you still did *not* publish. . . ?"

And then we heard again the odd buzzing noise from the hall below us, but louder this time and surely not of flies. Rather of some kind of apparatus. *And with it a loud scream!*

The old man nodded.

***

I'm almost finished (he assured us) but *there* is your answer. It lies in the pain. I brought the Irishman back to life, but the first thing he did when I did so was howl in anguish. The current coursing through his body -- it must have hurt dreadfully. And yet I kept it on, modulating it, turning it down to a tiny trickle -- his cries to a low moan -- but never having quite the courage to shut it entirely off. Rather I called back my fellow surgeons, having servants rouse them from their homes, from their very beds, to see this miracle I had accomplished. They, as I, agreed that unless I find some way to prevent the unimaginable suffering that this treatment necessarily brought with it, I should not publish a word of my findings. But also they agreed, even though the certificate be signed, that in that I had restored the corpse to life, it would be a violation of our solemn oath as physicians should any one of us endeavor to end it.

And yet . . . and I ask you now to remember what I said of flint hearts when I began this. And bankers and those of the legal professions.

For one of our number recalled the contracts. The contracts that each and every one of us had in possession, signed by this man's hand, willing to each the use of his corpse upon death for anatomical demonstration.

And, further, that Dr. M_____ had signed the death writ.

And yes -- *you hear him now!* -- that selfsame Irishman, that *Galvanic*, that resurrected-himself-Resurrectionist, his still living cadaver long since repaired of its trampling, laid on the table below in the Hall awaiting our presence. We will get him drunk first, before we cut him, to deaden not so much the agony of his dissection, but rather to quiet him lest his continuing shrieks otherwise interrupt the lecture. And then, once more, we shall repair him of any damage -- and some of the brighter of you may help us -- for he will be used again and again, as he has before, waiting the time between each year's new lecture, each new group of students, within his tub in the building's basement, the current turned down as much as we dare. But still with him always.

And so you have now a lesson of surgeons, what you will become yourselves. And you know now of their minds that can match wits with barristers' when it comes to enforcing contracts. And hearts of flint as stone-hard as bankers' in calculating the compounds of interest and drawing out worth to its final penny.

But there is another thing too you have learned now: A surgeon's faith in God. And in the life God grants to each of us, through whatever means, and the alternative lest you should think that keeping this man in pain as we do for repeated cuttings might tinge of cruelness.

He did, after all, sign a number of contracts, which to break would violate God's law as well as Scotland's; and, for all we know, he may also have at times committed murder. We do know he was a cheat, and a blackmailer. We know thus something of his soul's condition, you see, and what would become of it should we release it.

And that is the crux. We argued it, yes, throughout that whole summer, I often as not saying *"No! Let him die now!"* But I at last, also, was brought to consensus:

That this is our oath, as God is my witness, to heal the sick -- to bring the ill comfort in *soul* as in body. To pass on this teaching even as we are about to commence in the chamber below a few moments henceforth.

And, thus, what we do is an act of mercy.

Cinquains
Margarida Brei

Potter's Field
Lonely, scary
Burying, interring
Criminals entomb the unknown
Paupers' grave.

Common grave
Poor, sad, unknown
Entombing, roaming
The dead packed like sardines
Potter's Field.

The Majestic
Maureen Bowden

It stands, now derelict,
home to ghosts that roam
where once we surged through open doors:
a roaring horde of kids
that leapfrogged over seats,
filled the space with boos and cheers
to pierce the ears
of any god that ruled our sacred place.
Super Heroes, cowboys,
Doris Day, whip-crack-away.
The Deadwood stage evades the whooping Sioux.
Howard Keele's forte:
display of brawn in boots,
as baddies bite the dust to six-gun blast.

The hooves of spectral steeds still pound the prairie;
Wagons roll and rattle, on towards the west.
Meanwhile, darkened Gotham City streets
echo with the WHACK of Batman's fist
on Riddler's face.
The caped Crusader's footsteps tap a memory,
replay a long-gone matinée
in the haunted ruins
every Saturday.

Night of the Nine Jack-o'-Lanterns
Gary Davis

It was 9:30 on Halloween Night. Bill and Marianne were getting a little concerned as their three kids had not yet returned from trick-or-treating. Then, all of a sudden, their kids burst through the front door, panting and out of breath. They hastily dropped their trick-or-treat bags on the living room floor and quickly pulled off their masks and costumes. Brianna, the oldest, spoke first. "Mom, Dad! You know that old house up on the hill that you told us to visit tonight—the one with the nine jack-o'-lanterns out front?"

"Yes", replied Bill. "I thought there might be a lot of candy there for trick-or-treaters. Did you have a problem when you visited?"

"I should say so, Dad," said Brianna, shaking. Her younger brother and sister, Randy and Megan, nodded their heads furiously.

Brianna recounted what happened at the old house. "We knocked loudly on the front door and yelled "trick-or-treat!" There was no answer, so we knocked and shouted again. After waiting another minute, we peeked through the front windows, which all had shades drawn down. It looked like no lights were on inside the house. The windows also appeared very dirty, as if no one had lived there in a long time. Then we all walked around to the back of the house. Again, we couldn't see any lights on inside. We started to walk deeper into the backyard, toward the heavy woods at the far end. The wind started to pick up. It was blowing loudly from the direction of the trees. That is when things began to get scary."

"Yes", interjected Randy. "It got really scary out there and cold too. We thought we heard several faint voices saying, "Go away. Go away." Maybe it was just the wind.

But we didn't want to stick around to find out. We all ran back to the street in front of the house.

Megan chimed in. "We should have kept running all the way back home. But we stopped to look at the front of the old house one more time. The nine jack-o'-lanterns were all different. They had snarls and frowns on their faces. We shuddered. This was really weird. When we first got to the house, the pumpkins all had smiley faces and looked very friendly. How did they change to mean faces so quickly, especially if nobody was home? Did pranksters from some other house suddenly replace each of the nine jack-o'-lanterns while we were in the back yard?"

The kids' father spoke up. "Wow, that's quite a strange story." Their mother said nothing but gently shook her head and looked perplexed. Bill said, "I'm wondering about that wind you all heard. If it was blowing through trees, then maybe it sounded like strange voices. Also, the wind might have caused the lighted candles in the jack-o'-lanterns to flicker vigorously, which could have changed the appearance of their faces. They were all happy faces when I drove by earlier."

"Dad, I know what we saw and what we heard," insisted Brianna.

Bill cut her off. "OK, you kids go to bed soon. You can eat a little bit of your Halloween candy if you like. Don't eat too much, or you will get a stomachache. Your Mom and I are going to drop by that old house to see what's really going on there. Don't worry, we won't be gone for long. I was actually surprised to see any jack-o'-lanterns there tonight. I thought the house had been abandoned and quiet ever since old man Slater died ten years ago. I never saw anyone move in there."

Brianna said, "Well, be careful, Mom and Dad. There's definitely something strange going on. It isn't just a Halloween trick."

Bill and Marianne quickly exited the house and got into their car. They waved bye to their kids, who all showed concerned looks on their faces.

As Bill and Marianne drove through their town, they saw only a few jack-o'-lanterns still flickering; most had been snuffed out. There were no trick-or-treaters roaming the sidewalks. Halloween was almost over, they thought.

The couple soon reached the old house with the nine jack-o'-lanterns. It was situated on a heavily forested ridge just outside the town limits. They pulled up in front and got out.

Bill gasped when he saw the faces of the jack-o'-lanterns lined up on the porch railing. They were still burning brightly, as if the candles had just been replaced. The nine faces looked nothing like what he had seen when driving by the house early in the evening, on the way home from work. Every face was different—a frown or an angry scowl. There was now a strange individuality to each pumpkin visage. Before, they were uniformly smiling.

Bill and Marianne walked around the front and sides of the house, carefully looking at the heavily shaded, dirty windows. Again, as Brianna had stated, no lights appeared to be on inside. They walked up onto the creaky wood porch and rapped on the front door. No answer. Who, then, had put nine jack-o'-lanterns on the porch?

"Let's go to the backyard," said Bill.

"OK", replied Marianne. "But this place is already giving me the creeps."

It was a long walk towards the tree line in back. The yard sloped downwards a bit in front of the woods, since the old house sat on a ridge. The wind began to howl, like the kids had said. Bill and Marianne started feeling a lot colder; they began rubbing their arms. "Glad we got jackets," said Bill.

They listened closely for the strange voices their kids said they heard. The wind whistled in different pitches, but Bill and Marianne couldn't be sure they heard any words. They walked down to the very edge of the woods. The woods looked dense and forbidding, with lots of underbrush. It was a forest stretching way down the ridge. An almost-full moon could be seen peeking through tall oak trees.

Bill and Marianne began walking to their left along the tree line. They didn't see anything unusual. Then Marianne suddenly stopped. "I hear...something," she whispered loudly. "Somebody is saying, "Look, look." The voice is coming back from where we just started at the tree line, or maybe further back."

"Yes", said Bill. "I think I hear it too, but very faintly." "Let's retrace our steps," said Marianne.

The couple slowly reversed their path next to the woods. The mysterious, raspy voice—"Look, look"—grew louder. Another faint voice chimed in, also saying, "Look, look."

"I don't see anybody," said Bill. "Perhaps these voices are coming from trick-or-treaters hiding in the woods, maybe the same ones who put out the nine jack-o'-lanterns."

"I don't know," replied Marianne. "It's awful late for Halloween trick-or-treaters to be out now. And this place lies off the beaten path for kids where we live. Our kids only came here after you persuaded them."

Bill and Marianne soon retraced their initial path along the tree line. They continued walking in the direction of the voices, louder now. They began hearing a third voice, saying "Look, look closer." The couple peered intently through the dark forest on their left but saw no evidence of movement. Marianne remarked, "It's strange that we're not hearing any animal noises in the woods."

After a few more steps, Bill halted. "There's some kind of rise in the grass here. It looks big." Bill and Marianne shined their flashlights along the ground at the tree line. They could hear several shrill voices saying, "Look down, look down." Ahead of them, the couple spied a row of large bumps in the soil. Each bump was about six or seven feet long and rectangular in shape. They were lined up several feet apart. The soil in each mound had been lightly tamped down; there was almost no grass on top.

"Oh my gosh!", gasped Marianne. "These are graves. It's a row of six, seven, ...nine graves. They look pretty recent and like they were dug in a hurry. I don't see any tombstones or even wooden crosses."

Bill was shocked too. "Why would there be a new cemetery here? I don't think anybody has lived at this place for years. Maybe this was done to keep a secret.

Because of the way the ground slopes downward, you can't see these graves from where the old house is."

The wind was picking up and blowing colder. The strange voices picked up too. Now they were all saying, "Look down hill, look down hill."

The couple stared again into the heavy woods just down the hill from the graves. Again, they saw nobody. "These voices are coming from beneath our feet, from the graves themselves," said Marianne. "I think I hear four or five voices now, maybe more. They each sound distinct. Since we don't see anybody around here, these underground voices must be coming from...ghosts. Does that make sense?"

"Wow, you may be right!", exclaimed Bill. "I've read that people sometimes see or hear a ghost when the ghost has something important to communicate. Usually, something bad happened when the ghost was alive; maybe that person was killed or committed suicide. Whatever happened, it typically remains a secret. The ghost wants to expose the secret. He or she has a story to tell."

"Well, there must be nine ghosts here in all," replied Marianne. "Judging by how these graves are lined up closely in a row, the people here must have been buried at the same time. I'm guessing that they all have the same bad story to tell. The voices of these ghosts are suggesting that we need to find out what killed them. Then we need to tell that to the world of the living and reveal their secret."

"The ghosts are telling us to look down the hill," said Bill. "That means we need to look into this heavy forest. And there's lots of thorny underbrush here too. I'm glad we've got thick pants on."

Bill and Marianne gingerly waded into the dense woods below the graves. They shined their flashlights up and down and side to side. They ducked to avoid low-hanging branches. The couple could hear ghostly, faint voices behind them, still murmuring, "Look down hill, look down hill." Their movement forward and downward was very slow and halting; many of the trees had fallen.

Bill and Marianne walked about ten yards. Then Marianne began sniffing the air in the forest. "I smell something," she said. "There's a smoky odor in the air, like something got burned. It's getting stronger as we go downhill."

"Yes, I think I smell...Ouch!", cried Bill. They both stopped suddenly.

"What happened?", shouted Marianne. "Did you hurt yourself?"

"I scraped my ankle against something sharp," replied Bill. The couple shined their flashlights on the leaf-covered ground next to Bill's right foot. There was a little bit of blood on Bill's sock. "It looks like a piece of jagged metal," said Bill. He picked it up and inspected it closely.

"Be careful," said Marianne. "Don't cut yourself again."

After a minute, Bill said, "This used to be a piece of curved metal painted all white. Now it's almost entirely covered by black soot. So yes, you're right, Marianne. There must have been some kind of fire here."

"Maybe somebody hid a car or van in the woods and burned it up to cover up a murder or a bad accident," suggested Marianne.

"I don't know," said Bill. "If there were nine victims, that's an awful lot of people to stuff into a car or van. Perhaps it was a clown car. A lot of people hate clowns."

"Hey smarty-pants!", exclaimed Marianne. "Let's be serious. The ghosts can probably hear us. They didn't sound like clowns. They're going to get angry if we don't find out what put them in those unmarked graves. The wind is getting colder too. Maybe that is coming from the ghosts. Let's keep on searching. Does your ankle feel better now?"

"Yes, my ankle feels a little better," replied Bill. "The bleeding has stopped. You're right. We need to focus and keep looking down the hill."

The couple continued looking to their right, left and downward as they walked deeper into the forest. After two more minutes, Bill and Marianne stopped again.

"Oops!", said Bill. I almost stumbled over something big. It's not a dead tree."

"I almost stumbled too," said Marianne. She bent down with her flashlight. "This is a really big piece of white metal. It's very long and bashed in. Like that small piece you picked up, it's blackened a lot."

"This is too big to be part of a car or van," said Bill. "And it's too curvy to be part of a large truck. I don't think it's from a metal building or shed either." The two of them carefully stepped to the side and walked around the large piece of damaged metal. They both shined their flashlights forward, then stopped abruptly.

"Oh my gosh!", said Marianne, quivering in the cold air. "We just stepped into a big clearing. But it's not natural. So many trees have been knocked over. Everything smells burnt."

"There are big pieces of metal everywhere," said Bill. "This is a disaster scene. Look straight ahead, down the hill. There's a really long piece, with lots of little window holes in it. That looks like...part of a fuselage. You know, the central section of an airplane. I can see an airplane nose piece over to the left. There's a tail section to the right. That long thing we just walked around must be part of a wing."

"This is what the ghosts wanted us to find," exclaimed Marianne. "An airplane crash is certainly a big enough accident to kill nine people. But the strange thing is that I don't recall reading about any airplane crashes near our town, only auto and truck accidents. There should have been a story about this event in newspapers and on TV. Have you read about any planes going down nearby?"

Bill thought for a few seconds. "Actually, I did read about an airplane crash that supposedly occurred about a year ago in Richardson County, over to our west. Coverage of the crash didn't stay in the news for very long. Strangely enough, the papers said that nobody could find the crash site. The plane must have gone down in a heavily forested and isolated ravine. That county is big and very rural. There was a massive, driving thunderstorm the night of the crash, which explains why nobody heard it. Also, any fires at the crash site would have been quickly doused by the heavy rain."

"But that story doesn't make a lot of sense," replied Marianne. "People would have kept looking until they found the remains of the crash."

"Yes, you're right," said Bill. "But later, I read a long investigative report on that accident. The journalist speculated that the company making and flying the plane deliberately misled authorities about where the aircraft went down. The small plane was new; it was an experimental design. All of the crew and passengers were employees of the manufacturing company. This writer argued that the company wanted to hush up the crash story as soon as possible. The company didn't want bad publicity about its new aircraft design. Who knows? Maybe the company also paid the victims' families to keep quiet."

"Wow!", said Marianne. "That plane crash could have happened right here then. The company must have known that and sent out a team to secretly bury the bodies next to these woods. No wonder the ghosts are so angry. I see some numbers and letters on that big fuselage section. Those will help to identify this airplane. Let's take a picture of them with our phones and take pictures of other large pieces of the wreckage. We'll do a few photos of the graves also. We will show all these to the police. This is the beginning of a new investigation of a forgotten airplane crash."

After taking about a dozen pictures, Bill and Marianne slowly trudged back towards the old house. The burnt smell of the woods receded behind them. The air was still cold, but the wind had subsided a bit.

They turned around to look at the graves one last time. They thought they could hear a faint murmur of "Thank you" above the noise of the wind. The couple then resumed their walk back to the car. Marianne said, "Hey, what about the jack-o'-lanterns? There are nine of those here, just like the number of graves we found. That can't be a coincidence. Who would put out nine jack-o'-lanterns in front of their house?"

"That's a good point," replied Bill. "I think the nine jack-o'-lanterns are indeed connected to the ghosts we heard tonight. I was just thinking about the story of the original jack-o'-lantern. Jack, or 'Jack-of-the-Lantern,' was already a ghost when he began toting around his lantern. He had just died but was refused entrance into

Hell as well as Heaven. The Devil didn't want Jack in Hell because he had tricked the Devil earlier. The Devil gave him a burning ember to put in a turnip, later a pumpkin lantern. That way, Jack could see while wandering around in the eternal darkness of the Otherworld. Remember also that the world of the living is open to the Otherworld on Halloween. Restless spirits of the dead can therefore communicate tonight with people like us. The jack-o'-lanterns up front were no doubt intended to guide us to the ghosts in the backyard."

"But wait a minute," said Marianne. "The ghosts told our kids to 'Go away'." "Yes", Bill responded. "The ghosts were not in the mood for trick-or-treaters collecting candy. The meaning of Halloween for them is something very different. We were able to figure out what they wanted eventually."

"Well, I've had my fill of ghosts, airplane wreckage and jack-o'-lanterns for one night," insisted Marianne. "Let's go back home."

Bill and Marianne soon reached their car. They looked back at the nine jack-o'-lanterns before getting in. The pumpkins were still crackling brightly as if their candles would last forever. And their faces were all smiles.

Scifaiku:

we flip through the photo album
sweet whispers in the leaves
mother's apparition fades

Colleen Anderson

The Name-Us Game Counterpoint
Cecily Winter

He woke at his desk fully dressed and shook his head to knock the fog from his brain. His laptop screen glowed and he tapped it. Weirdly, it blossomed into the police sketch of Star Silver. Her real name was Kim, his first, and he still recalled her silken hair threaded through his fingers. Too bad he had to let her go.

He must've been tripping all night because he didn't recall leaving the house and trolling for the Kim lying curled under his cheap duvet. Over the years, he'd spent a fortune on bedclothes. DNA was a bitch, and here he was playing the odds again.

A curl of smoke he made out through a gap in the drapes told him he'd burned her clothes. He got up and twitched the drapes closed. He didn't want any peeping Toms or nosy parkers calling the cops. On second thoughts, the smoke could have been from the last batch of sheets. If they didn't ash up soon, he'd douse them with gas. Physical evidence had to be a no-show.

It was barely dawn. And the old stone farmhouse would be chilly until the sun got high and he could open the drapes. It was only the three rooms: his easy-clean bedroom-cum-living room, spartan in the extreme; the bathroom with lime-green fixtures his mother made his dad install days before she cut out; and the kitchen about which the less said the better. He'd long ago stopped climbing to the second floor. The roof leaked. It was a mess, but his dad's mess, and he was long gone. Found face-down and well-nibbled by foxes out on the old cornfield. Verdict—heart attack. Maybe the Devil squeezed it.

He pushed open the bathroom door. Like he figured: he'd been way out of it. Had he been roofied? He selected a packaged toothbrush from the vanity drawer and set it beside the sink then took a gray sweatsuit from the closet and folded the two-piece on the toilet seat as per usual.

The new Kim, still in her undies, tiptoed toward him hugging her arms tight about her chest. She asked, "Where'd you put my clothes, buddy?"

"Time to shower. You can wear the sweats."

She didn't argue. Baby in the sandbox. He liked them to argue. It raised the temperature.

No lock on the bathroom door, so steam billowed to his laptop where he sat spot-lit by a gleam of sunrise through the chip in the blacked-out transom. While he waited, he searched his mind for the place he'd picked her up. He needed the details for the record. Well, she'd tell him soon enough.

He pulled up the website of the National Missing and Unidentified Persons System. Since he first logged on to NamUs a while back, a bunch of Jane Does had been identified and labeled with their real names.

He didn't care for girlie names—Barbie, Juliet, Tiffany, whatever. After his mother took off, he'd been maybe five or six and went off the rails, stabbing and dismembering all her precious Barbie collectibles. He burned their clothes on the cornfield where he'd dug graves for the plastic corpses.

He always christened his girls Kim, but not all of them were blondes or shapely. Why not sample the sample pack?

He kept no paper trail, all his records were in his head—and only the date and city where he picked them up: Kim/May 14, 2015/Trenton; Kim/October 3, 2013/Jenkintown; Kim/February 7, 2000/NYC. He'd been almost 17 with the first. Made a mess of his truck—his dad was pissed—and he'd avoided major spillage ever since.

He rarely ventured far on a hunt, too much stress driving long-distance with doped-up hookers or, sometimes, chicks already dead from vomiting behind the gag or a too-tight chokehold.

When NamUs excised people, it meant they'd been identified, found, and returned in body bags to their next of kin or a potter's field gravedigger. He never read the newspapers to check on women he'd didn't know but he'd noticed a brief article last week on the hiker Kim/March 4, 2021/Wildwood. He preferred full burials but a scare from a cruiser siren forced him to leave her naked and exposed to the crabs and gulls between a couple of dunes. She was brand new on NamUs and captioned as Jane Doe with details of her coloring and approximate age. Only 15, though she'd acted older.

Cops had never turned up at his door, never questioned him once. His dad had taught him how to stealth hunt—squirrel, possum, crows—and one day if he got the chance, he'd take down a mama bear and her cubs. *Blam, blam, blam.* He chuckled. He didn't use bullets on the tender flesh of the Kims.

He flinched when new Kim's wet hair brushed his neck as she leaned over his shoulder. She wore his bathrobe. It swamped her. He glanced at the family photo at the rear of the desk—the last one ever taken. His shiny-cheeked Barbie-mad mother, his beefy dad with mean eyes, and him aged around five, when he was cute as a Disney grasshopper.

Kim had brushed her teeth but didn't smell soapy. Why didn't she wear the sweats he left out for her?

"This website your hobby," she asked, "helping the cops and families of those missing people?"

Her voice was rich and melodic, somehow familiar like she was the daughter of the off-Broadway chorus girl Star Silver, there to make his day with some special brand of whoopie. The pros always held out longer than any runaway teen thumbing a ride or slavering to bolt down a free meal.

"Keeps me engaged with life," he said, catching back a snigger. "I'm drawing a blank on how we hooked up. Where was that?"

She punted the question. "You ever crack a case?"

"You doped me last night?"

"Get real."

He eased closed the laptop. "Cracking a case isn't the point."

"What d'you mean?"

He had no answer she wanted to hear. "You need some joe? I got instant."

"Water's good. I'm parched."

"Sure."

He got up easily, limber as a cougar, and swept the cottage for escape routes. Windows nailed shut, ratty drapes still drawn, and the front and back doors key-locked and bolted high. In the steamy bathroom, a corona of soil rimmed the bathtub drain. The faucet trickled water into a Dixie cup. Faucet needed a new washer; maybe he needed to look for a new hunting lodge.

The farm he'd inherited from his dad went belly-up before he'd dropped out of high school. He didn't know how his dad made money, but they lived off the grid and he'd never wanted for anything. Got a second-hand truck for his 16th birthday. No cake though.

It wouldn't be hard to leave. The house was icy in winter, a fly-blown furnace in summer, and there was talk of an eminent domain taking for some highway to nowhere special. He wasn't planning to stick around if the bulldozers got busy. The place was a potter's field of tortured Barbies and sweet-sucker Kims. He'd wanted to lay his dad to rest there but couldn't risk interference from the local busybodies.

At his desk, Kim leaned on her elbows, with her fists punched into her cheeks. She was engrossed in the screen and didn't flinch when he crept up from behind in shoes with such a smooth tread they barely left a mark even in moist soil.

"Good with computers, are you?" he asked, crowding her, messing with her radar.

"Never used one before, but these faces popped up."

He frowned at the NamUs array on screen. Hadn't he logged off? It was spooky—all his Kims side by side like they were in a line-up to identify him. The notion tickled him.

"Any idea who they are?" she asked as he handed her the paper cup.

"Missing persons. There are thousands."

She drank the water in one gulp like the night's workout sucked her dry. He couldn't recall a thing about it, and her skin showed no visible bruises. He must have blacked out before the fun hit the fan.

She twisted a hank of hair around a finger. It had a silvery sheen wet. Not that she was old. She couldn't have been a day over 25. Maybe she'd had a fright and her hair grayed overnight. He'd heard it happened. Some lousy john or hopped-up street punk giving her the business. Well, she was lucky she landed in the hands of a professional. His business was elegant. It was art.

She leaned back in his chair. "You ever wonder if they're dead under a concrete slab or tractor-load of dirt? But I guess some are alive and keeping a low profile, looking for a way to get even."

"The living got better things to do than hiking down the revenge road. The dead don't care where they're at."

"You ever think about the stuff before, the brutality?"

"Philosopher called Hobbes called it right when he said that life's nasty, brutish and short."

"Well, you're a regular Mr. Congeniality."

"He saw the truth and told it."

He yanked Kim into his arms—she was a real lightweight—and lowered his mouth to nuzzle her cleavage. He let his hand slip along her inner thighs. He was aroused, but she wriggled away. Somehow put distance between them. She stared at him full-on with shadow-flecked eyes. Not the eyes of any Kim he'd met before.

"I better go," she said. "I'll take the money owed."

"Don't owe you nothing," he said, aware of the curl of his lips, his rising belligerence. "You didn't put out. You want cash, you better stretch out on your back."

"I didn't come for that, and I'm not clear how I got back here, but I know it's about Kim and a debt you never paid."

Star Silver Kim had happened to him twenty years back. Was Star new Kim's mom, and this whole roofie set-up was about getting even as she'd slyly implied? *Wow.* That *was* interesting.

"Convince me about that debt," he said, dropping into his chair. He dragged her by her hips onto his lap. With one arm hooked around her waist he worked the cursor to bring up Silver Star's face again. Her flatmate had handed the cops a professional-portfolio photo and reported her missing, but she hadn't known her real name and Kim had never been found. Her remains lay in a shallow grave about 200 feet east in the old cornfield. He'd never risked photos or videos, but he liked having her public portrait on call.

"You meant this Kim?" he asked.

Her hitching breath broadened his grin.

"What did you do to her?" she asked.

"You look like you're the imaginative type. Guess."

She struggled to pry herself off his lap, but he held her down even though she was squishy as a pillow, and slippery as if she'd smeared herself in liquid soap or melted fat. His heart muttered up a storm and he went all over clammy.

Performance nerves? He licked her ear. She tasted like dirt. "You're going nowhere, honey."

"That so? You think you can keep hold of me?"

"I know it."

"Tell me how many you killed, Mr. Congeniality."

"I'll bring them up if that's what you want. You won't be snitching me out."

She stopped struggling as if her predicament had upped and slapped her hard across the head. She overlapped the center edges of the robe. He didn't like her wearing it. He'd have to burn it when he was through.

She reached to tap the space bar, and that portrait array she'd been studying filled the screen. Fifteen photos or artists' reconstructions. He didn't like a hasty drop-off but it couldn't always be helped. Luckily the only found Kims to date were four outliers recovered out of state.

The re-visit juiced him, and he imagined hurting new Kim in the same slow, delicious ways he liked best. He hardly ever drew blood. She sat frozen on his lap, and he relished the dread settling in her heart, the fear feeding on her adrenaline.

The quick pressure on his inner thigh was exquisite, made him gasp with pleasure. Then his leg spasmed. He batted her hand away. The white terry robe was ruby red.

She'd hidden his razor blade in the robe pocket, damn her.

"Call an ambulance," he barked as he shoved her off his throbbing leg. She floated from him like a balloon caught in the wind. The pain was intense but why was he hallucinating? Arterial blood sprayed from his wound. How long did he have?

Hovering about a foot from the floor, she faced him and laughed. Only the first Kim ever laughed at him, but not after that first night. He gritted out the words, "Do. It. Now. Bitch."

She leaned close, stinking of the grave. She tapped the photo array and from the screen oozed figure after figure which solidified into some of his former playmates. And others he didn't know. They circled the desk. Some were matronly; he'd never interfered with anyone who might have been his mother. Then a change came over them. Their flesh melted until they were bare skeletons decorated with dangling shreds of sinew and hanks of brittle hair. Some wore rags. Those weren't his Kims.

His tongue clamped to the roof of his mouth. He wished he'd drunk that Dixie cup of water. Ten Dixie cups. The dead closed in, shifting through the desk and the laptop, squeezing him small as they lay their bones and smell on him. Some scratched and bit right through his clothes. Some stabbed his face with rusty nails. He winced and whimpered. What the hell was going on? A nightmare, right?

He lurched to his feet. He'd throttle the Kim who set him up, but his crippled leg folded and toppled him. Heavy with blood, the robe dropped over his head. He clawed at it. A rock or maybe a bone hammered on the base of his skull until the crack echoed through his head. The pain stunned him a while.

When he opened his eyes, the dead had retreated, their eye sockets empty, their jaws gaping.

"Thing is," Kim said, hovering naked beside him and balling up the robe, "these gals and I resent being stuck in the cornfield. We formed a posse."

"What kind of posse?"

"A vigilante posse. We're haunting serials, or hunting if you want to be precise. I used to be a regular housewife right here until my husband strangled me with my tights for the last time."

"No way. My whore of a mother ran off."

"She didn't run. She was wheelbarrowed off."

"If you are her, tell me my name."

He clutched his wound, tried to cover it with his warm, greasy pants. He was faint and wanted to throw up. He needed help. A mother had to help her son.

"I'd planned on leaving," she said as if telling her history trumped his actual damn life, "and I'd have taken you, but I forget your name after all this time, Junior. Once I'd clawed myself out of the dirt though, I sniffed you out in a heartbeat. You can scrub at yourself 'til the cornsilk flutters, but bad blood never washes off. If the cops stumble across your remains after we're done, you'll become a John Doe on NamUs. Or maybe the story will come out and you'll be one of a famous serial-killer duo: the Father and Son Cornfield Killers. Impressive, right?"

He grunted, couldn't spit out the nails he needed to hammer down her coffin lid. Maybe she never had a coffin out there in the family potter's field.

"Don't be sore," she said. "According to Hobbes it's 'kill or be killed.' Or is that the Neo-Darwinists? Whatever. Consider yourself selected out of the breeding game." She came to ground lightly and extracted his wallet and keys from his pocket.

He needed his ID and his car. He lunged but fell back sobbing.

"We need funds for stuff now the posse passes as human when the need arises. Sorry about that, but we figure you owe a lot of us and your dad owes the rest."

She squatted to tuck the blade between his right thumb and forefinger. "You know the right thing to do. It'll only hurt a little while. Isn't that what you used to tell them? Now, ladies, give him a chance."

He breathed easier with a weapon in hand. "Call the cops. An ambulance. I won't tell anyone you cut me."

She shrugged. "Only you can hear me. You going to finish this?"

He shook his head feebly.

"Okay ladies."

The dead crowded him. they stank of rot and blood and piss. Kim laughed. Was she truly his mother? If he could crawl upstairs, he'd check the family Bible, the strongbox of family records.

He played on her natural sympathy. "Mom, call an ambulance. Call the cops if you like."

His leg was all-over numb and his head was light enough to float away. He thought he might be having a seizure.

"It's a hoot, right, this Name Us game?" Kim said as she shook a finger at him. "You've been bad and your worst nightmares showed up to collect. I'm finished here."

Kim dragged her clothes from under the bed and began to dress. It had been a con, a set-up, a honey-trap. She didn't wear the flashy hooker garb he'd expected but a wide skirt, a crisp shirt, and canvas sneakers. She looked like she'd stepped out of a magazine ad for laundry detergent or hair dye. The image of his mother in the black-and-white photograph.

He murmured, "Take the photograph."

She didn't hear him. When she drew the drapes, he was half-blinded by the shock of light, the blood puddled over the floor tiles. His heart fluttered. His ears rang with screams. His own? The echo of theirs?

"Ambulance," he whispered, but there was only screaming, sharp and piercing, slicing through him, shredding him from the inside out.

Kim the mother disappeared, floated through the door or the ceiling or whatever in her human guise. Or maybe she stayed to watch while Ghoul Kim/July 12, 2007/Allentown, now in possession of the razor blade, squatted her hefty bones over his chest and very meticulously began to gouge his eyeballs from their sockets.

Vampire Girlz
Colleen Anderson

Vampire girlz walk slow, slouchy
dyed black hair long and lifeless
usually thin from denying life
more fragile than the break of day

Vampire girlz don't grin or giggle
cool as the grave, graver than dirt
night lace and wine dresses don't reveal
smudges should they touch the earth

Vampire girlz know they're drop dead sexy
deadpan looks keep the curious at bay
an ankh marks them for the unbelievers
they swoon Lestat deaths for all to see

Vampire girlz have soft bruised lips
sigh gothic words, love the strange
their skin is lead white from staying indoors
spending too many nights in make-believe

Treasure
Margarida Brei

The dead body was lying in Potter's Field.

The dead body would be buried where it lay. It would be marked with a small stone, not so much out of respect, but more out of a practical need to state there was a body buried there and it was necessary to dig graves elsewhere.

The gravedigger looked down at the body. Oddly it was lying in Potter's Field rather than at the gate, where bodies were normally placed. Sometimes clothing gave some indication of who the person was. A uniform indicated an unnamed soldier. Sour rags indicated a tramp. The gravedigger always felt it a great loss that bodies were unclaimed. He often wondered if the dead would remain dead on earth, having no one to claim them as family or friend. The body in front of him was dressed in nondescript clothes. She was youngish, neither pretty nor plain. There was so much blood, that the gravedigger nearly gagged. So very much blood!

Sometimes there was a treasure on the dead. Something overlooked by those transporting the dead bodies to the Potter Field's gate. Something the carriers dismissed as valueless was sometimes coveted by the gravedigger. A torn book, verses, a novella or a diary. He liked the diaries best of all, because they built up a character around the dead making them seem like real people.

The gravedigger held the lantern high. The body was still warm, although life had long fled. There was so much blood that he nearly fainted. In one way the blood was fitting because Potter's Field referred to Akeldama, field of blood. Indeed there was so much blood that he nearly missed the treasure. A baby! The grave digger realized that the woman had bled to death giving birth. The baby girl was truly a treasure, so he named her so. He hobbled back to his cottage holding Treasure against his heart.

The gravedigger had not spoken for years; speech was unnecessary as he was alone in the graveyard. There was no one to speak to. Only the dead entered Potter's Field. Visitors were forbidden. It could have been argued that the gravedigger communicated only through his flute. His music would ring out pure and clear in sad notes. However, he thought it appropriate to welcome the baby through soothing words. When the gravedigger actually spoke a few rusty words, he was so shocked that he nearly dropped Treasure. After a long draught of water, he spoke again. The words sounded creaky and odd. Then he began to sing soft sounding words. Nature had not been kind to him, but at least it had given him a beautiful voice.

In the morning, he returned to the dead body. He carefully went through her pockets. On a slip of paper were written two names in a childlike writing. The first was the name of a girl, perhaps the dead woman's. The second was a man's name, but barely legible as it had been slashed through several times by angry pencil lines. The gravedigger thoughtfully refolded the paper and put it into his pocket. As he dug, he looked at the woman. Yes, he thought she was neither pretty nor plain, but she seemed to have a kind face. Unfortunately, he was ugly. Rather than continue to be the target of every cruel joke or someone's whipping boy, he had decided to be a hermit in Potter's Field. Nature had given him an ugly visage; his hare lip distorted his asymmetrical features lending him a frightening grimace. His eyes too were mismatched, one was muddy brown and the other a startling lilac. Some fools thought he could look into men's souls with his lilac eye. Fools!

While digging, his shovel hit something metallic. Stepping down into the shallow grave, he found a few coins. Presently, he had no need for money, but guarded the few pennies he found. It was always judicious to be well prepared. Money meant little to him, because he was paid in food, clothing and other necessities. These were left just inside the gate every week. He never went into town to make a purchase; he preferred a solitary life and never left Potter's Field. The gravedigger was reasonably self-sufficient having his own well-tended vegetable patch, small fruit orchard, a goat and a few laying hens. The goat would provide Treasure's nourishment.

It puzzled him why the woman was found in Potter's Field. Why had she dragged herself there to die? Shame? Perhaps, having no ring, she was unmarried? Where was her family? What did the two names on the paper signify? Why was the man's name scribbled through?

Nature had been cruel to him, giving him a blatantly ugly face, a hunch back and club foot. The cruelest blow of all was giving him an acute brain. He had a very clever mind, but what use was it in a graveyard? His mind craved usefulness and stimulation, that gravedigging could not give him. However, he felt positive that Treasure would help him feel whole.

Before burying the woman's body, he took off her shawl and wrapped Treasure in it. After shaping the dirt around the grave, he said a few words. He had put more care and consideration into this grave than he had into any other. This was important. Every few days, he placed a small glass jar full of fragrant blooms. He also strangely enough began to speak a few words to the dead woman. As months passed into years, this became a sacred ritual. He always kept the graveyard clean and tidy and naturally spent time on maintaining a meticulous grave for the woman. He did this to honour Treasure and her mother.

All this heavy manual labor made the gravedigger very muscular. He had always had a sickly painful body and the extra strain of the manual work added to his agony. Strangely, after he buried the woman, he never felt physical pain again. In fact, his body moved with a new grace, almost a lightness. Was the dead woman thanking him in some mysterious way? The gravedigger never dwelt on this oddity. He was grateful, but he was far too busy. He was too busy to notice that his own singing once so melancholy and dull, had taken on happier notes.

There was such a freshness and joy about the gravedigger and Treasure that a few years rolled quickly by.
***

The gravedigger woke with a jolt. Something was horribly wrong. It was not the loud thunder which had woken him. Horrified, he saw the door open and banging in the gale. He knew that he had locked it before retiring to bed. Treasure? Where was Treasure? Grabbing his coat, he charged out into the night. Cold hard rain pelted him. He ran straight for the woman's grave knowing Treasure would be there where she spent so much time. A gigantic streak of lightning lit the sky and the graveyard. Even without this illumination, the gravedigger would have known exactly where to go. With joyful tears, he picked up Treasure and ran back to the cottage.

Under a bundle of blankets there was movement. With a shaking voice, the gravedigger asked the little face which peered out from the bundle why she had left the cottage.

In a tired yet clear child's voice, the answer was, "Mother called me!"

The gravedigger was shocked by this answer. A zillion questions buzzed through his mind, but he asked who the woman was.

The little voice merely answered, "She's my mother." Being extraordinarily bright for a three-year-old and realizing the inadequacy of the reply, she added, "I don't know who she was other than she was extremely poor. She always tells me that she loves me. Being poor she did not have the means to look after me. It was shame that brought her here to Potter's Field. Shame that she could not look after me. My birth has kept her tethered to the earth. She cannot leave because my very being keeps her here. She feels it necessary to keep me safe."

On hearing the child's words, the gravedigger realized just how very mature Treasure was. Perhaps the mother had gifted the child wisdom. He realized too with a sigh, that the dead woman would hurt neither of them. Then he thought of another pressing question.

Love Unto the End
Colleen Anderson

To Aphrodite

Let me know love, unending need
Never let me starve or want
But gift me with the greatest hearts
Still beating, burgeoned, full of vigor
Where flows life's blood surging
Speeding on with infinite dreams
Vitality so copper rich and hot

With each one you place upon my path
Let me know them and their heart's desire
Of fixing knots upon their finite threads
And when I reach to know them better
To release each one of life's fetters
Let me hold the meaty pulsing heart
Taste the textures of their final thoughts
Their pain, their complex never ending fears

As I drink the flavors of each precious being
Let me be thankful for evenings caped in dark
Adore the stars that watch me in my dance
Let me never feel your burning curse
Jealousy or spite of my immortal lover, Night
Or face the spurning hatred of the sun

I will in turn revere and love you endlessly
Continue to adore you for this wondrous gift
To always love intensely what I do
To understand and honor every soul I take
To always savor memories of each sacrifice
To love them best, their throes from life drained

Who?

Mike Morgan lives in Iowa with his wife and two children. He spends a lot of time staring off into the distance. People think he's daydreaming, but he swears he's thinking up stories. Rumors that he's actually asleep at the keyboard are (probably) unfounded. If you encounter Mike in the wild, try distracting him with cheese or craft beer. Don't, under any circumstances, start talking to him about science fiction or you'll be trapped there for hours. If this sort of nonsense doesn't leave you rolling your eyes, you can find him on Twitter as @CultTVMike, or you can read updates about his latest publications on his website: https://perpetualstateofmildpanic.wordpress.com

Colleen Anderson is a Pushcart nominee, and has received Canada Council and BC Arts Council grants for writing. Her works have appeared in numerous venues such as *Polu Texni, The Future Fire* and *Cascadia Subduction Zone*. She edits anthologies, writes fiction and is working on two collections of poetry and a novel.

James Dorr is an Indiana writer specializing in dark fantasy and horror, with forays into mystery and science fiction. An Active Member of SFWA and HWA, Dorr has been a technical writer, an editor on a regional magazine, a full-time non-fiction freelancer, a semi-professional musician, and currently harbors a Goth cat named Triana. An avid reader of non-fiction as well as fiction, including histories of such topics as early medicine, Victorian funereal practices, and past scientific theories, Dorr counts among his major writing influences Ray Bradbury, Edgar Allan Poe, Allen Ginsburg, and Bertolt Brecht.

Denny E. Marshall has had art, poetry, and fiction published. Some recent credits include cover art for *Bard & Sages Quarterly* April 2021 and poetry in *Eye To The Telescope* April 2021. In 2020 his website celebrated 20 years on the web. Also in 2020 his artwork is for sale for the first time. The link is on his website. (Direct link is www.dennymarshall.net) Website is www.dennymarshall.com.

Gary Davis enjoys exercising his imagination through crafting dark and darkly humorous poetry and stories. He particularly likes classic supernatural horror. In poetry, imagery of the senses is especially important; poetry is a form of painting within Japanese Zen. The topic of the unmarked grave in *Potter's Field* recalls the famous Poe horror story, set deep in ancient catacombs—"The Cask of Amontillado." It is also important to convey a sense of the loneliness and silence of the unmarked grave within a vast natural universe.

www.ingramcontent.com/pod-product-compliance
Lightning Source LLC
LaVergne TN
LVHW011848060526
838200LV00054B/4224